Katrina, Della and Me

and Other Stories

By the same author

Salamanders

Katrina, Della and Me

and Other Stories

Pete Murphy

AESOP Modern Fiction
Oxford

AESOP Modern Fiction
An imprint of AESOP Publications
Martin Noble Editorial / AESOP
28 Abberbury Road, Oxford OX4 4ES, UK
www.aesopbooks.com

First edition published by AESOP Publications
Copyright (c) 2019 The Estate of the late Pete Murphy

First edition 2019

ISBN: 978-1-910301-65-4

About the author

Pete Murphy was a true original: a highly gifted writer steeped in the tradition of Hemingway, Chandler and Elmore Leonard, but with a voice distinctively his own – caustic, subtle, and with a disturbing and sometimes explosive edge behind its understatement.

A Vietnam veteran, until Hurricane Katrina in 2005 Murphy was based in New Orleans. As a result of the hurricane he lost everything apart from his cat Della – including his home, all his possessions and even the manuscript of his novel *Salamanders* (published by AESOP Modern in 2018), which fortunately he had previously sent to his editor. After Katrina he moved to Garland, Texas, where he worked as a carpenter and decorator before creating the old time radio website, otrdepot.com. He died in March 2011.

Murphy's experience of Katrina, together with a number of his short stories, are recounted in this book.

Contents

1	Katrina, Della and Me	9
2	Bennie	33
3	Closing Up	55
4	First Kill	67
5	Orville	81
6	The Parakeet	111
7	Annie and the Mick	119
	Appendix I Notes on the Stories	171
	Appendix II Notes from the Basement	175

1

Katrina, Della and Me

September 6, 2005

It was a dark and stormy night. No. Actually, night and half.

The morning was okay, till five-thirty. Then all hell broke loose. It was like God or the devil really went and did it this time, pissed somebody off real good, found their match. Something finally got between them and not a goddamn thing they could do about it...

Half the roof blew off, shook our building hard. Later, when the dark left, we'd find its pieces in the parking lot and seven cars pretty beat up, each with at least three windows blown out or two-by-fours stuck through them. The water had covered our tires. A friend on the street behind us was not so lucky. His car was almost completely submerged.

Meanwhile, as the wind and rain continued – after the roof blew off – I heard water in the front room. I was on the second floor. The rain had gone through the third floor and into my ceiling. The ceiling light was gushing water. I switched it off and put a trash bucket under it.

Then another drip started. For about half an hour I emptied buckets into the bathtub. Then it got too fast and part of the ceiling came down so I gave up bailing and turned my attention to the other room, and Della. I cut huge contractor's trash bags and covered her with three layers of the stuff. So far that room was not leaking. Then the rest of the ceiling came down in the front room.

The phone went dead, then the lights, then the water (they'd apparently shut down the pumps). Now the whole area was black and the wind was screaming. The next-yard tree came down on our fence and into our yard. All we could do now was wait and wonder what was happening.

Daylight came through about nine o'clock. That's when we could see the parking lot destruction. The first floor apartments were thigh deep in water. A lot of trees were down, roofs of month-old homes torn off.

About two p.m. we got brave enough to wade to the levee and walk down it. The storm seemed to have passed.

We lived on what is called the 17th Street Canal, the border between Orleans Parish and Jefferson

Parish, supported by levees and higher concrete sea-walls on either side, sheets of iron inside the concrete. We were the first building on the Jefferson side in that block. The tops of the sea-walls are about 30 feet above street level, surely high enough the canal could never overflow no matter how much Lake Ponchertrain rose, no matter how much it rained.

We walked down the levee.

Lake Ponchertrain is a little less than a mile from us. As we approached, we saw the Orleans sea-wall shudder and a section give way, letting the canal water (which is Lake Ponchertrain) into Orleans Parish. Then another section fell, and another, and suddenly about 500 feet of the seawall fell and Lake Ponchertrain blew itself – (downhill) – like a tsunami into Orleans and ripped up 200 year old Oaks and covered fine old homes in minutes. I mean *covered* them! Three story homes – poof-disappeared. Orleans had become a basin and was now becoming part of Lake Ponchertrain. Nobody in those home had a chance.

They never knew it was coming.

A wide stream of fire shot up from the water about 50 feet high. Apparently from a gas main under a street now probably 20 feet below the waterline. It was still burning hours later.

We were very lucky the break did not happen on our side. We thought about that for a very long time that day. I know we all did.

* * *

No electricity, no water, no phone, no cellphone chargers that work from car batteries. (Incidentally, my car survived only a few dents in the roof and a spidered windshield. Fortunately, I'd just gotten a new inspection sticker the day before. I'd been again lucky.)

First thing I did was hook a hose up to one of the water heaters and call for big pots. We filled a couple crawfish pots and some smaller ones and had water good enough to drink if it got serious but certainly plenty of water for rinsing stuff off, including ourselves. We had 18 water heaters. The guy behind us with the sunken car was a good scrounger. He knew a lot of neighbors and gathered a few gallons of water and a bucketful of soft drinks, then a huge brand new never used gas outdoor cooker with side burners, and then, from another source, a couple tanks of butane. I'd just bought about 30 pounds of chicken thighs from

Sam's Club and it needed to be pulled from the freezer and cooked. I'd also gotten broccoli and baby carrots and romaine lettuce and strawberries and grapes. So we hauled the cooker to the second floor and cooked and cooked and cooked and ate and ate and ate.

That was Monday. The water in the parking lot was still tire deep. It was not going down. Somebody had a portable radio. We found out that the guys who run the pumping stations were told to evacuate with the others. Bright idea. Only in Louisiana, the lowest education in the nation, next to Mississippi. The water did not move all day. None of us knew if our car engines and/or their computers were okay.

Daybreak Tuesday I was up and gauging the water level. It was going down now about four inches an hour. I sat in my car and listened to the radio. No way I could get to Belle-Chase – my new job – anytime soon and now obviously no good place to get to my job *from*. When the water was low enough I checked my oil and transmission fluid for yucky stuff that shouldn't be there and started her up. Beautiful sound. It was then I decided to get out of dodge as soon as possible. That would probably be Wednesday. The news was anybody that could get to 1–10 could head west.

That was me. Go west young man.

Wednesday morning I gathered up Della and dungarees and t-shirts and socks and underwear (Hanes boxer-briefs, if anybody's curious), my huge Sam's Club box of Tide, four pillows, 2 quilts for sleeping on, and a telephone for Della and headed for Baton Rouge.

I got there at nine. First stop, Regions Bank. Pull $1000 from a credit card to checking account. Two rolls of quarters. Second stop, get a newspaper.

Payphone local calls there are fifty cents. Some of the calls needed a dollar. No vacancies. Already rented. No we cannot change our one year lease and deposit policy for evacuees. No monthly rentals. No vacancies. Already rented. Decided to try refugee evacuee for a while.

That didn't work either. I'd wasted my time and almost two rolls of quarters pissin' up a frozen rope. At 4 p.m. I headed west again. Head west, young man. Next stop, Lafayette.

The traffic in Baton Rouge – cars and people – had been unbelievable. Some gas stations already dry of gas. I suspect the town will experience a gigantic boom and in a few years be like living in a nightmare. I'm already glad I didn't hang around.

By the time I got to Lafayette I'd decided to gas up both tanks and keep going. I found a simplex nail in my front tire, pulled it out, heard the hissing, stuck it back in and headed for a repair station. I'd been very lucky again.

It was almost dark when I got to "Lake Charles – next seven exits."

Every exit looked like the worst neighborhoods in New Orleans. Getting on and off the interstate so much I somehow wound up in a place called Westlake, obviously west of Lake Charles, the lake and city both, and decided to find a place to sleep. A guy told me to check the Recreation Center. Not hard to find. The town's about a mile and a tenth long with one main drag, one supermarket, three gas stations and little else of any great importance. Driving in, I saw a lot of industrial plants of some kind.

Anyway, the folks at the Recreation Center were great. Showers, swimming pool, handball courts, workout gym, game room, etc. Free towels, soap, food, etc. I opted for what to me at the time was their best offer: Drag a mattress anyplace in the basketball gym I wanted. The air conditioning felt full blast. I loved it. I totally crashed.

Thursday morning. Newspaper. Street map for Westlake and surrounding areas. Another bunch of quarters. For some reason I decided I wanted to be in Westlake, not Lake Charles. I don't know why.

The lady at the Rec. Center counter copied the exchange locations from the phone book and I concentrated only on them. Couple hours later I found one about two blocks away. The maintenance man was there now and he'd show me the place but I need to go to Sulphur to apply for it. I checked it out. Great apartment. Better than the one without a roof and 2/3 the price. Omigawd! Central air. Never had central air in my life. A dishwasher, even. And no dishes. Maybe I'll wash my socks in it. Month to month rent. I headed to Sulphur. West again. Head west young man.

At Dredd Properties Inc. in Sulphur, on September 1, 2005, at about 11:00 a.m. I fell in love with Michelle.

It is now 8:20 p.m., Thursday night. Della is purring. She likes it here and keeps asking about her phone line. I keep telling her the #$%&@ Bell South phone company apparently cannot handle the load and that I keep dropping quarters into the box a mile away and it keeps telling me to try again later. She pouts. I tell her I will try again in a couple hours and will keep trying every two hours until I get connected. She coos at that. I know how to handle women.

* * *

1:00 a.m. Friday. Well, I'm not going to tell Della this, but Bell South has 9 to 5 regular business hours like every other business, half day Saturday, closed on Sunday. I surely expected, since they're as essential as electric and water to so many people, they'd be accessible 24 hours a day. Neither rain nor snow nor sleet nor hurricane ... oh.

Wrong folks. I'll try again in about 8 hours. I expect the phone message will again be "all circuits busy, try again later."

9:00 a.m. Friday. Sure enough, same message. Somebody here suggested that the 1-888 Bell South number for residential service, though national, needs to be routed through New Orleans. I doubt that.

Rather, I doubt they'd not have bypassed that system this long after the hurricane, especially knowing there are evacuees that need service transferred to a new higher and drier location. If they're relying on the old system I'll not have service till New Orleans does. Possibly months. Jeesh.

This morning I bought an ash tray and toilet paper at the Dollar General. Gave my name and order at the Rec. Center for free prescription refills donated by Walgreens. I should have padded that order. Drugs. I *need drugs!*

Reconned Sulphur this morning. Much bigger than Westlake and more businesses. *Huge* Walmart's. I suspect Sulphur is where everybody from Westlake comes to shop.

Word is, people will be allowed back into Orleans and Jefferson on Monday and Tuesday to check on their stuff. I might go back to pick up more stuff and anybody who wants to get out. Need a real tune-up and two front tires before I go. I don't see the tune-up happening here and tires are likely to cost big time. Mull mull mull.

1:00 p.m. Found a guy off the beaten path who looks well-equipped to do a good tune-up but is too busy today, doesn't work weekends and wants labor day off. Suddenly my luck doesn't seem to be holding. Might have to trust Ophelia can make it with the tires and spark she has.

I'm wondering if anybody outside SE Louisiana would have any luck contacting Bell South to get my service connected. Still the same national number though. Dunno. I'll mull that over. Might be worth another half-roll of quarters to find out.

Can't seem to get much forward motion going today. Guess I'll drive to Lafayette, see if I can see luck.

6:00 p.m. 150 miles later Ophelia seems to be grinning about her brand new front tires. Scratch another hundred-fifty bucks. The peace of mind is worth it. On the way back Ophelia kept trying to tell me the speed limit is 70 and I kept trying to show her we're both too old for that. I'm a 55–60 mph guy with a now 70 mph babe. I told her I'd spark her up, get her wired up real good soon as possible. She seemed to consent and obeyed my right foot after that. I know how to handle women.

Lafayette seems to be a big town with everything a big town ought to have. Shame I couldn't have gotten a place there. But Westlake is fine. If it wasn't such a small town I'd probably not have gotten so lucky so fast.

Saw a huge convoy of semis w/flatbeds loaded with gigantic lighting equipment and generators headed for Orleans. Not a government truck in the bunch. The big question on all the radio stations today is why, five days later, the armed services and domestic services still have not responded properly. We can airlift anything to anybody anywhere in the world and can airlift thousands and thousands of people out of any place in the world yet there are still thousands of hungry people – including newborns – stranded and dying in Orleans. Probably a moot question that'll never properly be answered.

Just heard Haliburton will be handling the cleanup and electric problems. Hmmm. Mull mull mull.

Bell South is closed for the holiday weekend despite the problems in this part of the nation.

When I got back I topped off the tanks. Scratch another fifty bucks. Seems like only a couple months ago we hit two bucks a gallon.

Now it's two-sixty-nine for regular. Why, after spending billions and billions of dollars saving Kuwait and Iraq and Saudi Arabia, etc. from themselves, are gas prices going up and up? I doubt that one as well will never be properly answered.

People make the world happen but sure don't get much help with the chore.

Saw a Bell South truck on Sampson Street today (the main drag).

Next time I see one I'll have Ophelia herd it like a Border Collie.

* * *

Saturday 09/03/05 5:00 a.m. Forward motion might be stalled for the weekend. Don't know what else I can do except think about the ride back to Orleans Monday, get gallons of water to freeze. I'm sure they're okay with canned and dry foods down there. Maybe get a couple cartons of cigarettes. Sure hope somebody's got some bucks in their pockets. Need help with this project.

Mail down there will also be backed up for weeks. They need sorters. That means electricity. And gas for their trucks. Really need to get &*%^! Bell South waking up, get my internet, e-mail my boss, try to get my last work check sent here. Hope they didn't mail it pre-Katrina. Argghhh.

Was hoping to get internet access by now, do my online payments.

Four bills need attention before the 9th. Three banks and Allstate car insurance. Allstate office in Sulphur. Bank One here in Westlake. Handle them Tuesday. Get the other two to the post office today and hope they make it. Wonder if Bank One can take those payments and forward them electronically? Worth trying. Mail won't move till Tuesday anyway.

5:45 a.m. Already getting bored and antsy, unable to help forward motion.

Decision making in Orleans, as usual, is yo-yo-ing. Just heard nobody will be allowed in on Monday at 6:00 a.m. to check their homes and/or get people out, a complete reversal. That decision bounced back and forth three times yesterday. Nobody there should be able to run for elected office unless fully educated elsewhere and can do a comprehensive book report on See Spot Run.

7:00 a.m. Found the post office. It's on my street. Very handy. Mulberry Street. Oh the things that I saw on Mulberry Street (Dr. Seuss).

9:00 a.m. Now it's okay to get into Orleans at 6:00 a.m. Monday. I'm sure traffic at the border will be crawling. I'll probably leave here at 2.

12:00 noon Managed to get my bills handled. Broke again. Zilch in checking. The money blew up pretty fast. Shame about my job. Took me a long time to find something I was sure would be steady and secure.

I'd've had all credit cards paid off within a year. Oh well. That's why God invented credit cards.

2:30 p.m. I have discovered the Library, also on Mulberry Street between me and the post office. Very convenient. Free access to the internet twice a day. Closed now. Will reopen Tuesday. Maybe I can do BellSouth.com to get my phone hooked up.

Definitely check in with Storytalk. Wish I had Snow's e-mail address.

The main industries here are the oil refineries and casinos.

Reconned Westlake a bit. Discovered the Calcasieu River. Haven't fished much since I left the Oklahoma woods thirty years ago, but if I lived here I'd sure get a rod and reel, relax by the water.

Sunday 12:30 p.m. Went to Sulphur, got candles and cigarettes for my mission to Orleans tomorrow morning. I'm now on a personal boycott of Circle K. While all major companies have their regular gas set at 2.69 a gallon, All Circle K's in both towns have their regular set at 3.09. I never use their tiger pee but now I won't even use their stores.

Anxious about my mission tomorrow. Hate not doing anything. I'll need to force myself to sleep a bit between now and then, otherwise I won't sleep at all, just lie awake wishing it was 2 o'clock.

The idea of eventually moving here permanently has started creeping into my head. I'm not paying it much attention yet. There's plenty of time. A lot can be said for cheaper rent, nicer apartment, slower town, river half mile away. The other side is there's going to be carpentry work galore down there.

All things pass. I've lived with that idea most of my adult life.

It's kept me whole.

2:00 p.m. 12 hours to go. I keep watching the clock. If I still drank beer I could maybe go to a local bar, get somebody to knock me out. Beer sure was an expensive lifestyle. Glad I'm over it. (6 months).

The only "drugs" I do now are Ashwagandha, Gingko Biloba, Cordyceps, Kava, Eleuthero, and St. John's Wort. And age. I like where I am, mentally. I do not want to go through youth's anxieties again.

As you can see, I'm already so bored I'm talking about myself instead of reporting facts as seen by this Katrina refugee. Need to stop that.

2:30 p.m. Started to clean eight-year-old dirt off my once creme colored printer and speakers. Seems unproductive but I'm doing it anyway.

Monday 1:00 a.m. See you in about 400 miles.

* * *

Monday 2:30 p.m. Mission accomplished.

Boy that wore me out. Worth it, though, if only to make sure my mail will be collected and my stuff will be safe for a while. Brought all my kitchen stuff here.

The trip was mostly uneventful. Night driving scares me a bit – the glare and the nitwits behind me who constantly travel with their high-beams on – but I did 50–55 mph all the way and the wave passing me was always only 5 or 6 cars and 5 minutes apart. They'd closed I-55 East to only vehicles helping with the hurricane recovery and we detoured to Highway 61 south which became Airline Drive about 10 miles later and came to a complete halt. It was 4:30 a.m. and about 30 miles from where I needed to be: Lake Ponchertrain at the 17th Street Canal.

We sat for 2 1/2 hours. The Jefferson Parish border was about 14 miles away, so I guess that's how long the line stretched in front of me. They didn't open till 7 a.m., instead of 6 as planned. Once the line got rolling it was smooth sailing. Soon as I got to the parish border I turned left toward Metairie. It was a ghost town. I saw one other truck besides mine. Apparently all others in front of me in line were heading to other parishes. Armed national guard (boys, actually) at every major intersection. No traffic lights. Trees and poles and the bigger signs were down. Roofs gone. I didn't need to stop at all until I'd reached my apartment building.

Two had already left. The others still wanted to stay. I dropped off their frozen drinking water and candles and cases of soft drinks, collected my kitchen stuff and headed back.

I didn't stop all the way West, just did my 55–60 mph mode and liked the daylight. The waves passing me were now about 20 cars and semis each but about ten minutes apart. Tractor-trailers sure can buffet that van.

Ophelia amazed me. We'd never done a highway trip together. She did the whole trip on a tank of gas. A 1991 Ford Clubwagon loaded with tools (compressor, table saw, etc., etc.) She did about 25 mpg. I never would have expected that. Grand old gal.

Tuesday 09/06/05 10:30 a.m.

Well, my "Katrina-week Report" comes to its end now, my adventure resting on a somewhat ungraceful and anti-climactic picture: me – still broke and still happy to be above ground and whole

– in my boxer-briefs staring at a lot of kitchen stuff to clean.

PS I washed dishes and stuff for 45 minutes before remembering I now have a dishwasher.

September 7, 2005

My boyhood friend in Philadelphia managed to connect to Bell South. I'll have a phone this Friday. My next problem is waiting for New Orleans to get its postal service and internet running so I can know what my next move will be. If I can find work here I might stay. I already have an offer to go to Texas and work on an internet writing friend's houses.

I love change. I'm used to it.

September 8, 2005

My boyhood pal in Philly (Bing) managed to contact Bell South. Phone will be hooked up tomorrow. Another hurdle jumped. Still trying to get through via e-mail to my job so I can get my final checks. Also need New Orleans postal service up and running so I can catch up on my mail. When I know those things are cleared I will make one more trip down there to pick up books and winter jackets, etc. and try to sell the bed, tables, etc. for whatever I can get for the stuff. Nothing sentimental there, just functional.

I've pretty much decided to move on. I've spent more years in New Orleans than any other place in my life, including Philly, where I grew up. Time to see how other folks live, new territories, new adventures.

Definitely do not want to do a major city. They're okay for shopping, not for living. In a way, I miss my Oklahoma woods – the creek, the rabbits, the squirrels (yum yum), the solitude. Katrina probably had a lot to do with how I feel now.

All things pass, sometimes not often enough for our own good. Hitch-hiking 10,000 miles 35 years ago never gave me a chance to stay in any one place for a comfortable length of time. I might try Texas now. I will not wear a cowboy hat. Didn't even wear one when I played country-western onstage. These modern day millionaire country stars who wear them look downright silly and durned disingenuous.

Update on Orleans: Pumping out a slow process. Only 23 of 148 pumping stations operating. Work hampered by sporadic gunfire. Once all are running they can pump about a half inch per hour, a foot a day, given the estimate needed to be removed. Starting to see tops of buildings initially covered. Pentagon sending 5,000 troops from the 82nd Airborne Division with small boats, including inflatable Zodiac craft, to launch new search and rescue effort. (Hmmm. Running kinda late, eh?) About 10,000 estimated to still be in the city. Natural gas leaks. Government tests confirm sewage related bacteria ten times higher than acceptable safety levels. More than 100 died in a dockside warehouse while awaiting rescue.

Cadaver dogs now in use where water has receded.

Poland, Austria, Norway, Honduras and others have been waiting for U.S. approval to send aid and supplies. In Sweden, A C-130 loaded with supplies has waited four days for approval to take off.

Another sad note: Water now containing sewage, heavy metals, gasoline, etc. now being pumped into Lake Ponchertrain. (I'm wondering if the pipes are big enough to hold a body).

* * *

Note to self: Time to move my checking to a nationwide bank.

Regarding the gunfire here: I'm reminded of the education level/firearms mindset. A few years ago a 10 year old kid was arrested for killing another kid with a pistol. His response: "I didn't mean to kill him. I just wanted to hurt him a little."

7*September 16, 2005*

In 1996, when U.S. Senator Mary Landrieu, aka "Katrina Mary," and Kathleen Blanco , now governor, heard on election day that they were running behind in the polls, they sprang to action. It was 3:15 p.m. The polls were due to close at 8:00 p.m. Within forty-five minutes they had thousands of people in buses – music blaring from loudspeakers – heading through the streets to a free red beans and rice dinner. They won the election.

In 2005, on Friday, Saturday, and Sunday, – before Katrina – buses sat empty and high and dry while thousands looked for ways to get out of town during the declared evacuation.

Senator Landrieu has said – on national TV – that FEMA is at fault because they did not send buses to get people out.

New Orleans is notorious for its corrupt and indicted or convicted officials, including a governor, a state insurance commissioner, and many others. A senator now under investigation, while surveying the area in a helicopter with the national guard, had them bring him by his house to gather some items (while nobody else was allowed to check on their homes). The FBI has found bags of money in his freezer.

And now ... the federal government has said it will send billions of dollars here to rebuild the area. The officials here, of course, will be in charge of how the money is spent.

September 18, 2005

Phase three completed. This trip was more relaxed than the last, mainly because I-10 west is now completely open and today's permanent re-entry is restricted to a specific part of Metairie: between Kenner and the 17th Street Canal, my district.

Picked up my winter jackets, etc. and my books, now curled and water-stained and mildewed, but still in working order. The words did not fall out. Since I had to leave room for the stuff I brought here in phase two, I could take nothing else. I left the furniture. No big loss. Until I find my permanent abode I'll need to be somewhat mobile, like the seventies all over again. Who knows? I might decide to become the Storytalk carpenter, take care of all Texas then head north to Canada.

Anyway, phase four is "waiting for my mail to catch up with me."

When that happens I'll advise the landlord, have the phone transferred again, disconnect the electric here, and head west young man. Headin' yer way, Texas. Look out. Yahoo. Giddyap Ophelia.

2

Bennie

One day, near August, after they got settled down real good, Bennie Scudder asked April if she wasn't getting bored with him after three years four-and-a-half months.

He told her "You need to get off your ass, maybe work a little, get out of your rut."

April dipped her pork eggroll into the Chinese mustard and bit into it, nodded, her eyes widening, tearing up. "Yeah. Wow. That's hot. Yeah. Maybe help with the bills while you keep looking for work. Wow." She wiped her eyes. "That's hot."

He watched her bite into it, saw her eyes water. She snorted a little, tried not to cough, grinned.

He said, "Yeah? What's hot?"

She told him. "Every time you bring this up I think about it again." She dipped the eggroll back into the mustard and sniffed it a little, licked it, stared at him.

He stared back. "I said that before?"

"Yeah. You got a way with words, Bennie."

He asked her, "Fuck's that mean?"

"Means I love you, Bennie, that's all it means."

"Yeah?"

"Yeah, Bennie. You're my peach. You're all I got."

He stuck three fingers into a hole in his undershirt, scratched, stared at her.

She dipped her eggroll back into the hot sauce, asked him: "How about you, Bennie?"

"How about me what?"

"You asked if I was bored with you. Ain't *you* bored with you? You don't *do* anything. When you *go* outside, it's just to go get beer and come right back."

"I go to church. Sundays, I go to church. That's important."

"Nice, Bennie."

He stared at her a little more then closed his mouth and scratched the yellow highlighter she'd given him back and forth hard across a tiny spot on the newspaper.

"I got one," he said.

"What do you have, Bennie?"

"A job."

She wiped her fingers on the towel, asked him, "When you start?"

"Goin' over there Monday," he said. He got up and pulled a beer from the refrigerator. "First thing Monday morning."

She said, "That's nice, Bennie. Maybe next weekend we'll go back to New York, do Fifth Avenue, visit the relatives in your new underwear."

He sighed loudly, looked at the back of her head for a moment, then scuffed toward the doorway.

"Where you going, Bennie?"

"Outside, blow the stink off."

"To the bank? Open an account?"

He didn't stop, told her "Yeah. Single account."

The front door closed quietly. She shoved the eggroll deep into the mustard pot.

* * *

Sunday, after mass, Tom asked Bennie if he wanted to help round up an old boar he'd seen up northeast of the valley.

"Ain't seen him in years," Tom said. "Figured he was dead, or in somebody's fence-up years ago, but he's up there. Saw him yesterday when I was markin' shoats."

Bennie didn't understand. "You don't keep your pigs shut up?"

Tom smiled. "No, Bennie. Here in Oklahoma if you can't afford the feed you let 'em loose, give 'em free range, let 'em eat the hickory nuts and acorns, root in the woods. It's all lumber company property anyway. They don't care."

"Oh."

Tom looked at him a long moment, said, "Figured I'd take him over t'Antlers tomorrow, run him through the stock sale. Do that once or twice a month, gather one up and sell it. Helps me buy feed and other stuff I need."

Bennie nodded, said "Oh," again.

Tom watched him a moment. "Come by my place in an hour. I got a horse you can ride."

"Sure," Bennie said. "I rode horses up north. Ten bucks an hour through the park. Did that a lot. I'll come over. I got nothin' planned today. Might be fun."

Tom grinned. Bennie left him there.

* * *

April hummed. She put her sketchbook and her charcoals back in the drawer, went back into the kitchen and finished her dishes humming an old song she could not remember. She checked the refrigerator for her milk and the single cabinet to the left of the sink for her cans of tuna fish and Campbell's mushroom soup and boxes of macaroni. She shook the breadcrumb can, listened to it carefully then put it back. She filled her two quart pot with cold water and set it on the stove but did not light it. She hummed something from her Joni Mitchell album but could not remember some of it and drifted into a Perry Como song, then "Young Love" by Sonny James. She dusted their bedroom bureau and changed the sheets, folded their clothes on the bed and set them neatly on the shelves in the small closet. Then she stopped humming and sat on the bed and looked through her wedding album again.

Bennie came in, rummaged around the bottom of the closet, found his old hiking shoes.

"What you doing, Bennie?"

He sat on the bed, pulled off his sneakers.

"Got a job."

She closed the photo album, kept it on her lap.

"That's nice, Bennie. Really. What're you gonna do?"

"Help Tom."

"What're you gonna do?"

"Help round up a pig up in the woods. You know."

"No. What's that mean?"

"Oh, we gotta go find this pig and get it down to his place so he can get it over to the stock sale in the morning." He jumped up, kissed her on the cheek. "Gotta go," he said.

The door slammed.

She touched her cheek. Smiled.

* * *

Tom lived three miles further up the valley road and two miles north off the old lumber trail. Bennie drove slowly, but the dry silt of the road billowed up anyway and hung in the air behind his old pickup, quitting only at the little wooden bridges. The rains had washed the last two bridges apart but the creek was low now and the crossing easy. He crossed the winding creek five times before he reached the house.

Tom was already out by the road. He had both horses saddled, a piebald and a roan. Their reins hung loose to the ground. The taller one, the roan, stayed close to the warped hickory fence and poked its nose at Tom's shoulder. Tom held it under the mouth and rubbed its head between the eyes and watched Bennie drive up. The piebald lazed across the road chewing at thin grass. Some of the dogs had already gone up the road. Most of the others were lying in the road. Two were in the woods at Bennie's left. They all turned their heads and looked at Bennie as he walked up. None of them wagged their tails or barked.

Tom handed him some chaps and watched Bennie fumble with them a little then helped him with the straps.

"Helps keep your legs from gettin' chaffed too much, especially when the trees get too close in on us."

"Tom Mix had furry white ones," Bennie said.

Bennie could just see over the saddle. He watched Tom mount the roan then grabbed the horn with both hands as Tom had done and climbed onto the piebald's back. He gathered the reins and quickly got both hands back on the saddlehorn and sat straight up looking over at Tom.

Tom smiled. "Don't pull at the reins too much," he said. "And no need to use your feet. Just keep them in the stirrups. He'll know the way and set the pace."

The dogs who'd been up the road disappeared into the trees. Others didn't go up the road at all, just walked straight into the woods. Three stayed close to the horses. After they'd crossed the creek once and ridden a mile Tom turned the roan into the trees. Bennie could not see the other dogs. He still had not heard them bark.

"They know where we're going," Tom said. "They're working. The horses and the dogs are bred to work. They know their jobs."

One of the dogs, a white and tan, stayed close to Bennie and the piebald. It had a wide six-inch scar on the right side, down close to the belly. Bennie asked Tom about it, what was its name.

"Hog got her rolled over. They go for the belly. Had her in the air and shaking his head before the other dogs could get hold of his legs and make him fall. Took her home and stitched her up. Wasn't real sure she'd make it. None of them have names. They're just workdogs. My wife calls her Lucky. Lucky Dog. Lost three last year. The good ones stay alive."

Bennie let go of the horn. He felt much better about the piebald now. It had become easier, ducking under the lower limbs, pushing through the thinner ones and letting them snap back behind him.

After a while they got to the creek again but didn't cross it. Tom turned east along its edge and the ground began a gentle rise. They came to a small clearing and stopped next to a small shed made of saplings and brush built between two trees. It was open on one side and faced away from the creek. Straw covered the ground inside and a few feet around it. A bale of hay sat in one corner.

"He may have been here this morning," Tom said. "The feed I put out yesterday is gone. Could've been the sows, though. Hard to tell."

"You built that?" Bennie asked.

"Yeah. I got a few spread around. All within a couple miles around here, wherever the banks are lowest so they can drink. Their rooting takes them miles away looking for the hickory nuts and acorns but they come back to this area for the feed. Kinda keeps them located."

"Like they feel somebody's taking care of them?"

Tom laughed a little. He said, "Yeah. I guess."

Lucky Dog sniffed inside the feeder shed.

"How come I don't hear the dogs?"

"This is where they work. They'll bark when they need to. They're trained not to scare any stock might be around. They know I want the boar today.

They'll pick up the scent now and let us know when they find him."

Five minutes later the dogs started barking in the distance. Both horses got into a quicker lope and kept away from the trees wherever they could. Lucky Dog started to howl and the other two joined in. Bennie pressed his knees in hard against the piebald's shoulders and held the loose reins up against his chest. He did not want to grab the saddlehorn again.

The ground heaved into a steeper rise. Bennie leaned forward in the saddle as the horses moved a little faster to make the climb. He threw his right arm up and grabbed a branch and pushed it over his head. His arm hooked a brier that wouldn't pull loose and he stretched the arm back to free himself. The brier dragged along the arm and slipped off. The horses were not slowing. A hickory branch lashed across his face. His body jerked forward in the saddle as the rise quit and the ground flattened out again. Tom slowed and listened.

The dogs were howling now and closer, somewhere in the hollow to the south.

"I see him," Tom said.

He cut the roan to the right, down the steep slope. The piebald followed. Its hindquarters dipped. Bennie shoved the stirrups forward and held his body back with his arms rigid, his hands back at the saddlehorn again. At the bottom the horses slowed to a walk.

The boar was thirty feet from them now. The dogs had him in a circle and spinning as they yapped and barked, snapped at his legs. The boar's squeal seemed almost a roar now. Thick saliva frothed around his fat pink tongue and dripped from his three inch tusks – two up, two down – and shot into the air as he spun. Clumps of the heavy spit stuck to his matted hair. He lunged at each dog in turn as he spun and his glaring old red eyes seemed unable to widen enough. They kept snapping open and shut quickly as if to rid themselves of the water that had now built up in them. His old legs seemed too short now for the massive red bulk they carried and their hooves slipped on the pine needle blanket of the forest as he lunged and squealed and lunged again, spinning.

"Jesus," Bennie said.

Tom was off the roan, unlashing the ropes.

"Get down," he said.

Bennie climbed down.

Tom slipped one of the lariat coils onto his left shoulder. He took the other one in both hands and eased the noose out wider with his right.

"They won't get him down," he said. "Old boy's too big, too smart."

"How we gonna do this?" Bennie asked. His feet were on the ground now but his hands still gripped the saddlehorn. He kept staring at the boar.

Tom looked over. He smiled at Bennie, then walked toward the boar. "First we got to get him down, cut those tusks so he can't hurt nobody," he said. "Come on."

Tom got the first rope around the boar's head on the second throw. He ambled to the left, keeping the rope loose, and wrapped it around a thick hickory, tied it off. The dogs moved as he moved and gathered on the left side and front of the hog. Tom got the second rope around the thick neck and eased over to the right. He gave soft and quick commands. The dogs stayed at the left. Tom tied it off to another tree and called Bennie over.

"Hold this end. When it starts to straighten, ease some out. Keep it wrapped like I have it and ease it out slow, maybe a foot at a time."

Bennie's mouth was open. He nodded.

Tom went to the other tree and untied the rope, started pulling the hog toward him. The dogs slipped back. Bennie's rope was off the ground and straightening. He eased some out. He felt no tension in the rope but his knuckles were white and his hands sweated in the grip. The hog tried to back off but Tom held tight and pulled him closer. He gave another soft command and the dogs moved off to the sides a little. Bennie eased out more rope. Tom's pull was steady, firm, gentle. Tom gave another quick command and the dogs quieted. The squealing seemed louder now. The boar's head was low and at the hickory now and Tom wrapped the rope three times and tied it off.

"Snug yours up. Not too tight," he told Bennie. "Then tie it off good."

Bennie did as Tom had said and quickly pressed his hands to his ears. He stared at the old boar screaming, at the fat swollen blue tongue, at the wet old red eyes. He dropped his arms when Tom came over.

Tom said, "Okay, get him down."

Bennie stared at him, his mouth open.

"Get him down." Tom did not smile.

Bennie shook his head.

"I think you need to do this. You'll be okay. Go get him on the ground. He goes down, he won't get up."

The squealing was inside Bennie's head now, trying to push itself out through his ears.

"You'll be okay. Just don't get your head near his legs. You need to do it."

Bennie approached the boar. Tom gave a low command and the dogs made a wider circle, getting Bennie in it. As he got nearer, the circle closed. Bennie watched the tongue, the tusks, the eyes. He lunged and slammed his chest into the boar's side, tried to get his arms around but couldn't do it so he kicked into the dirt and pushed but the hog stayed up and Bennie switched his arms and reached under and grabbed the opposite rear leg and pulled with his arm and pushed with his chest and his feet and the boar went down.

Bennie didn't move. The hog stayed down.

Tom walked around the hog, came up facing Bennie, held out the cutters.

Bennie looked up at them and rolled onto his side, looked up at Tom.

Tom smiled down at him, almost whispered, "Do it."

Bennie grabbed the cutters and slipped his body toward the big head. He saw the one big crying eye stretching itself back, trying to look at him, the squeals coming louder and faster now, the old boar panting, screaming as Bennie reached and cut, trying not to hurt the swollen purple tongue but knowing now it did not matter anyway and cut the second one and then the third, screaming with the old hog now, both of them screaming and Bennie trying not to cry as he cut the last tusk out of the old bleeding mouth.

Bennie rolled away. He sat up panting. Sweat crawled over his face. He had saliva in his hair and on his face. He held the cutters limply at his lap. The dogs laid down, quiet now. Lucky Dog came and laid next to him. He looked up at Tom.

"Like that?"

"Just like that," Tom said. He smiled.

Bennie looked away.

* * *

They left the hog lashed to the tree and rode back and got Tom's stake body. Tom drove the old lumber trail and came around behind the hollow and close to the hog. He had to cut three trees to get the old truck in there. They used the ropes and the dogs to get the hog up the ramp and into the bed. Bennie helped Tom slip the gate into place and lash it to the sides. Coming back the hog kept butting the sides and the cab with his head. The squeals were much quieter, almost tiny whimpers. They sounded strange coming from a boar that size. The old truck rocked and pitched with the rough ground and the heavy hog butting like that. It was a rough trip the whole way back. It took a long time.

* * *

By five o'clock they'd gotten the horses out of the corral and the hog was running its fence. After a while it slowed to a trot and made one more round then stopped at the far end.

"He's broke now," Tom said.

Tom and Bennie climbed the fence. Bennie pulled the hose over and filed the trough, watching the boar. He was not moving anymore and his squeaky noises had stopped. His mouth was wet and bloody and his tongue hung out. His panting slowed and his eyes were tiny slits, watching Bennie.

Bennie went and stood next to Tom at the fence.

"He's pissed at you," Tom said.

"I broke him," Bennie said. "He ain't free no more."

"He did all right," Tom said. "He must be nine years old. I turned him loose seven years ago, then lost him."

"How much longer would he live?"

"Three, four more maybe. But he'd be too old for anything then. The wolves'd get him."

"But he'd be free."

Tom looked over. "To do what?"

"Something. Anything. He'd be doing something."

Tom eased himself off the fence. "Just keep eatin' up the hickory nuts 'n acorns is all." He walked toward the house. "I need them for the sows."

A woman and two little girls had come out the side of the house and Tom went over and talked to them across the fence. Bennie looked over at the boar. It had started walking toward him. It started to trot, then got up to a good gallop, coming at him. Bennie kept one hand on the fence, but didn't move. The boar kept coming, its eyes wide again, not tearing anymore, clear, the big head up as it galloped faster now and Bennie didn't move. It ran until its legs buckled six feet away and fell forward into the dust.

Bennie walked over, knelt down. He put his hand on the big chest. It was still. The eyes were open. They did not look old.

Tom came over to the boar to make sure it was dead. His wife watched from the fence. He told her in his soft voice to call some help.

"We got to get this butchered," he said.

He looked over at Bennie leaning across the fence at the far corner of the corral.

* * *

Neighbors came and the men hoisted the huge carcass and got it hanging from a high a-frame in the corral close to the kitchen back door.

Kids came and took turns with the hose as Tom cut the skin away. He had fast hands, a butcher's hands. He trimmed the fat and honed the long knife with a long rod hanging from his belt.

The women cleared the three big wooden tables and got them into the kitchen shoved together and covered with newspaper.

The kids washed the meat as Tom cut it and carried the pieces into the kitchen and the women laid them out across the tables in stacks according to the cuts.

The men stood by and kept the conversation going.

"Had to be an eight hundred pounder."

"More like nine."

"Six hundred dressed, you think?"

"Sure. An easy six."

"Sold that boar to Tom nine years ago for eighty dollars and a wink."

"Nine years. Imagine."

"It was a shoat then, 'course. Litter of eight."

"An eight litter. You always had good sows."

"This one was real good. Give me six litters 'fore I quit her."

"That was his mama," one kid told another.

"I knew he was good when I sold him to Tom. He had spirit."

"A good sign. Always a good sign."

Bennie stood back and watched, listened, watched the cutting.

When Tom had finished they all crowded into the kitchen. The meat covered the three tables and was ready to wrap in individual pieces. Some of the stacks were over a foot high. They were all silent for a moment, staring at the tables.

Tom turned to Bennie, grinned, said softly, "Looks pretty good to a poor man, don't it?"

* * *

It was almost eight at night when Bennie got back. His going out had taken up the day.

He set his box of wrapped pork steaks and soup hocks on the table as April came in from the bedroom to greet him.

"Bennie, honey, you look worn out." She brushed his hair back off his forehead, kissed him on the cheek.

"That's my pay," he said, pointing at the box.

She studied him. "You okay, Bennie?"

"Yeah. I stink."

"Let me run a bath for you," April said, "and you can tell me about your day."

"My day was about pigs and dogs."

She kissed him on the cheek. "Let me run a bath."

He stared at her a moment. He shook his head, clenched his eyes to get the water out. "The good ones stay alive."

"Let me run a bath." She kissed him on the cheek again and started for the doorway.

"No." He rubbed his cheek. "I'll do that. You put this away. Make sure the freezer's okay. Maybe defrost it first, get the old ice out. Make room in the bottom section first, take the shelf out, get the box in there so it stays cold, then do the freezer. Make sure you get that old ice out of there."

"Okay, Bennie. You okay?"

"I'm fine. Just make sure that meat don't spoil."

He walked into the bedroom and took his clothes off, left them on the floor.

April said, "What is all this, Bennie?"

He told her, "Pork."

He turned the shower on, got it hot.

"Steaks?" she called.

"Yeah, some of it. Might be tough. It's from an old hog," he yelled, and stepped into the shower.

* * *

Bennie woke at daybreak. He got up quietly and slipped into his hiking boots and dungarees, grabbed an old undershirt from the hamper, pulled it on and went into the kitchen. April was still asleep.

He got a towel off the drainboard and held it under the water until the temperature felt just right. He wrung it out carefully, making sure he'd left it wet enough. He sat at the table, took his shoes off and wiped the mud, then got up and rinsed the towel and cleaned them again, getting through the old crust, finding the leather. He studied them, rubbing here and there, scraping now and then with his fingernail and rubbing carefully. He looked at them closely and at arms length, then closely again. The leather had a warm, rich glow. They looked newer now.

He put them on, stood, tested them, felt a newness in them as he bent his knees testing them, down and up slowly, down and up again. He smiled and walked toward the doorway and back to the table. He did that again, nodding to himself, smiling, walking.

He walked into the bedroom and found a new dungaree shirt on the closet shelf. It was still in the box. He looked through his tee-shirts and found one that looked white and had no holes. He walked back into the kitchen and laid them carefully on the table. He pulled off his undershirt and stuffed it far down into the paper trash bag.

After he'd put on his clean tee-shirt and the new shirt with the pockets and buttoned it up he walked to the front door and went outside, see if he could find something to do.

Maybe bag up some hickory nuts and acorns, make a little feed site in the woods along the creek where the bank was low.

3

Closing Up

It was almost ten at night when Jessie Whaler watched the last car in the next block pull away and turn the corner. Her little street was empty now. The whole town had gone to the big annual celebration at the lake. It was her birthday, but this year she didn't cry. This is my day, she thought, and surely I deserve some special time with it alone.

She drew a deep breath and stretched her arms and clasped her hands together feeling very wicked and tingly now, excited and private about it. She went about this business of closing up carefully and with an arousing sense of guilt.

She thought about that for a moment and decided no one really needed her little bar now, most especially tonight. Some will have gone home already, their heads cloudy from the drink, their stomachs churning the spareribs and the spicy hot crawfish and the corn and boiled potatoes. Most would still be at the lake long after midnight, alone or clumped in tiny groups discussing how much

better their little towns' picnics had gotten with
every year.

She stared at the empty street for a moment and
thought: Three years, daddy. I've kept the place
running three years now since you died. You're
proud of me, I know. 'Course we don't have all the
business like when you were here, but that's okay. I
like it quiet. Quiet is always better.

First she locked the door and lowered the blinds
in the two display windows so she could really be
alone, careful about letting the slats slip down
behind her plants. The streetlamp scattered little
shards of light into the bushes at her curb. An
incredibly stupid looking dog trotted up to lap water
from a pot near the door. He bounced to the bushes
and peed, then looked at Jessie a moment and
wagged his tail. He smiled. Jessie smiled back.
Satisfied, he sauntered away, skipping a little as he
walked. When he trotted too fast his left rear leg
pawed the air three times quickly like a pumphandle
before hitting the ground. The other legs somehow
paid no notice. He was deaf. She had named him
Crank.

There's no need to rush this, she thought. She had
plenty of time for the closing up. She liked that. She
lit a cigarette. The fan circled slowly overhead,

whirred at her, bounced the smoke in slow motion eddies against the walls.

She began with the bar, wiping it slowly. She had already done this twice today, but she liked her bartop, the oldness of it and the scorings in its wood that spoke of other times, other hands, other quiet broodings. She was a little girl then, and remembered now having sat on it while her father tended to his friends. She remembered the explosive laughter and her silly giggling within it.

It was very quiet in the bar now. She swept the floor clean of cigarettes and ashes. There was not much of it. She picked up an empty crumpled pack and threw it in her wastebasket. She gathered up two glasses and a bottle from one of the booths, brought them to the sink behind the bar, then went back to wipe the table. She went to her bedroom in the back and brought out her can of room freshener and sprayed it around. It smelled of baby powder. Much better now, she thought. Smells good, huh mama? Your little girl's having a birthday! You and daddy watch me, I know. That's why I have a fine life here. You still take care of me.

She went behind the bar and began wiping down the bottles, reading the labels, arranging them just so, and paused at a bottle of brandy. I think I once had some of this, she thought. She stared at it.

"Well," she said loudly, then put her hand to her
mouth and whispered "Shhhh...", then quietly, a
finger to her lips, "Why not? It's my birthday." She
saw nothing wrong with having a little celebration
of her own. She got a clean glass and poured a little
of the brandy into it. She let the first sip sit on her
tongue, keeping the glass to her lips. It tasted sweet
and tickled her throat as it eased down and the
steam of it inside there somewhere made her need to
choke but she suppressed it. Her eyes watered now
and the sticky liquid eased down into her stomach.
She sipped the rest of it.

She said "Well" a little louder, startling herself.
"That's much too sweet." She drew half a glass of
beer from the tap and drank it down. It cooled her
throat. She giggled and finished wiping the bottles
and the shelves and the mirror behind the shelves as
far as she could reach. She stared at herself in the
mirror. Then she cleaned the glasses in the sink and
threw the empty bottle to the trashcan. It missed and
clattered into the corner. She went and picked it up
and dropped it into the trashcan and covered it with
the lid. "Stay," she said, then winked at herself in
the mirror and went back to finish at the sink.

She spoke to her plants and watered them and sat
on one of the stools checking the room again now to
be sure everything was correct. I've done a good job

here, she thought, and went back behind the bar and picked up a bottle of Old Grandad, filled half the glass with it, and went back to her stool. She drank half of it quickly, grinding her teeth together as the strong whiskey rushed down her throat and warmed her stomach. Her eyes watered again and she wiped them with her forearm.

She whispered a low "Wow" and finished the rest of the whiskey and slammed the glass down onto the bar as she'd seen her father's friends do it before he died.

"Good party," she said. "Damn good party." She giggled her little girl giggle and spun herself on the stool with the giggle. The bartop looked cloudy now and she decided it needed wiping again. She bent over the bar and got her rag, started to wipe. She couldn't wipe the cloudiness away and began giggling again. "It's my eyes," she said, and laughed the way she'd seen the old men laugh, low, deep, tossing her head back with the laugh.

"This is a good place," she said aloud. Crank watched her through the door. "Come in," she mouthed to him, "it's my party." Crank grinned at her and scooted off.

She sighed deeply and went behind the bar and poured herself another half glass from a different bottle and filled it almost to the rim with beer.

"Now I believe we are having a good party," she said, and drank half of it. She went back to her stool. She saw Crank watching from the doorway and pretended not to notice. If I ignore him, she thought, he will want to come in.

Crank scooted off.

She turned on the stool and stared at the pieces of her face behind the bottles. She grinned. The grin crawled, bent with the old glass and fragmented between the bottles. She laughed and bowed her head.

"Hey, Charlie."

Charlie didn't speak. He was a scrawl in the bartop. Jessie moved to the next stool. "Aggie. You a whiskey drinker, Aggie? You need a fill-up? You know Charlie?" She glanced toward the door. Crank watched her. She got up, went to let him in.

But he'd gone. She laughed again.

The fan circled overhead.

"I am having a damn good time here!" She yelled, and laughed again. She went behind the bar and got a shotglass and a bottle of whiskey and filled a new glass with beer and brought them all to a booth she liked because you could see the plants easily.

She spoke to the Swedish Ivy hanging in one corner of the display window.

"You havin' fun, Nora?"

She poured some whiskey into the shotglass, trying hard not to let it overflow, but her hand shook and the whiskey sloshed over the rim and spread across the table and onto her lap. She wiped the white cotton dress with her right hand and bent her head to sip from the shotglass.

"Nora, you gotta try to be more vocal. Don't let George bother you." She looked at the cactus sitting in the clay pot under Nora. "You look like a little dick, George. A little dick with pick-me-ups on it." She giggled and tossed the rest of the whiskey down and poured another. "Pick-me-ups like what you get on your socks walking through weeds." The whiskey puddle grew. She looked at the other plants.

"You girls enjoyin' my party?"

Silence.

She looked toward the bar. "Hey Charlie! Come on over here. Sit by me."

Silence.

"Awww, come on, Charlie. You don't love me? Yer gonna miss out Charlie, you don't come over. You might get lucky."

She drank half the beer, wiped her lips with her forearm. "Had a lotta men tell me they love me, Charley, so don't go thinkin' yer sumptin' special. How about you, Aggie? Wanna get lucky tonight?

You guys want me to come over, sit on the bar like I yoosta? Sit with my legs tucked under, my knees out like chicken wings? I'm a big girl now, guys."

She finished off the beer, winked at Nora. "A lotta men." Crank came to the door. She pulled herself up and went toward him. Her head swooned. Her eyes lost focus. She braced herself against the jamb and looked down. Crank had gone.

She staggered back and plopped down hard into the booth and wiped her face with her hand. She felt very warm. She stared at the shotglass.

"Fergot t'drink that one."

She slipped her bottom lip over the top one as far as it would reach, held it there and looked around.

"All right all you people, ya gotta go. Yer too fuckin'loud. Get yer asses outta here. I need some silence in here. I gotta have a little time to myself. Gotta have it quiet now."

She giggled, then double-checked her closing up chores. Door locked. Lights out. Back room out. Front light out. Fuckin' street light on. Need a gun. Could shoot it out right from here. Across the street, bam! Ha! Gotcha. Lights inside. Two little red ones and a puny thing over the register. Good. Door locked. Lights out. Juke box off. No sounds. Surrounded by no sounds. No lights. No sou...

Keep hearin' a tick. Where th'fuck's that at? She looked around the dark room. Goddamn clock. Fergot t'turn the clock off.

She laughed out loud. Her voice echoed a little in the room.

Y'don't turn a clock off. I heard it before. It ain't a tick. It's a hum. Been listenin' to that fucking hum for an eternity. What I need is silence. But there's a hum. A drone. A ... whirrrr...

She looked up at the fan. She pursed her lips as far as she could then stretched the sides out slowly, sloowwwwly, and wound up with a grin. She grinned at the fan, winked at it. And she knew. The silence was at her fingertips. Somewhere. She looked around, squinted her eyes, and tossed the whiskey down. She shut her eyes tight and hard and her mouth curled up with the taste and she set the glass down gently, searching for the table with her eyes squinched shut then opened them fast.

The room brightened for a quick moment. Two switches. Gotta be that one. The room darkened again. She pushed herself up and strode awkwardly to the front door. Two switches. Both down. Fuck's that mean? Means two things are off, dummy. She tried one anyway. The outside light went on and off as she played with it. The other one was the lights in the window-seats. She pursed her lips again, moved behind the bar, sneaking now, her shoulders stooped, grinning at the fan, peeking at it with the corner of her right eye, careful not to look at it directly.

She found the other switches at the other end of the bar, above the white crème de menthe, just inside the stairway wall. Three. She couldn't remember ever shutting the fan off. She stared at them. One was the stairs. This one. This is the back room. This is ... she couldn't remember, and didn't really want to be wrong. She pulled her hand away. Her foot slipped on the wet cement floor and she fell, hitting her right elbow on the sink and skinning her forearm against the sharp Formica counter as she dropped.

She sat for a moment and stared at the pipes and the bucket under the sink.

"Gettin' very wet in my seat," she said to the bucket. Her arm hurt. She started to rub it and knew it was raw. She pulled herself up and leaned into the sink. The cold water felt good along her arm and she bathed it up to the shoulder, letting her short sleeve get wet. She turned now, eyed the switchplate, tried her grin on it. She sneaked toward it. Her left arm shot up to the switch and she grinned hard, ground her teeth as her fingertips swept down and...

The juke box went on. Nothing was playing. The last song had finished. The room lit up too much. She straightened and leaned against the wall with her left arm and swung up and around with her wet right one and shut it off.

The fan continued to whir at her.

Then she saw it. And knew everything would be all right for ever and ever. She had control. It would be all right now. The tiny cord hanging from the fan looked like spider's silk. The fan whirred at her.

She whirrrred back at it, and climbed onto the sink. She started for the bartop. Her right foot slid on the waxy surface and her left one buckled and now she was losing it, falling back and down, her arms flailing, her shin scraping the sink edge. She fell back into the shelves. Bottles and glasses crashed to the floor with her. Her head spun. The whiskey smell enveloped her. Darkness tumbled down. She was blacking out.

She cried "No!" and pulled herself up, crying "Not yet. Not yet". She got to her feet. This time she knelt on the sink, then crawled to the bar top and began to stand, stretching her arms out as far as she could. Her legs shook. Her right arm was still the best, cut or not, she thought, and she lashed out with it, caught the slender cord between her fingers. She started to fall and grabbed quickly with her left, but too low with it. She pinched hard with her right hand fingers, felt the cord burn through them. She knew she was going over the counter now but didn't give a shit anymore because the fan was stopping, it was slowing, she was falling...

Her body twisted with the movement and she landed on her right shoulder and the right side of her head.

She stayed very still. Mainly because her head hurt, but mostly she was listening for the fan. She barely heard it. It was stopping. And now ... she'd locked the door. And the lights were out. She could shut her eyes and there would be darkness. And no whirrrr. She'd beaten it. It was her world now. Whatever she wanted to make of it. She shut her eyes. Safety. She'd locked the door. Darkness. The floor felt cold. No more whirrr. Silence...

...just the tapwater still pounding into the aluminum sink.

She pulled her knees up to her chest and wrapped her arms around them, buried her face there. Her bottom lip pushed itself out over the top one. She began to cry and lay there with her cheek in her tears on the cold floor a long time before she fell asleep.

4

First Kill

"He won't be here," she said. "I know it."

The rains had come and gone and come again. They had been sitting on the slopes for over an hour pretending everything would be all right. The sun had crept into the valleys and beyond the tree lines and the hills behind their blind but not yet reached them.

Silver fog floated among the trees and between the rocks into the dark caverns of the hills and out again, down into the ravines and up, hugging the pine-needled forest floor, sniffing, searching. Bubbles of blackened water rose from the mulch and popped into the mist, pushing it a little, as if trying to shove it away. But the fog merely hunched its back a little – seemed to smile with thousands of tiny unwavering shrugs – and moved on.

"He won't be out in this rain," she said again.

"Be quiet," he said. "He'll be here. He won't mind the rain."

She sighed a little and thought about laying the rifle aside, but remembered his anger about things like that and kept it across her lap, under the poncho. The cold late November dew had been chilling her bones for almost two hours now and thinking about the kill only made her muscles stiffer. She prayed for the sun to hurry, prayed for the fog to pull itself up.

"He'll sense us," she whispered. "He'll know we're here."

He shook his head.

After a while she asked, "When I shoot him, will he be dead immediately?"

"Don't ask that again," he said. "I've told you. Don't think about that. It's not something you need to think about."

She shivered a little and pulled the hood farther out over her face and watched the rain dripping onto the poncho covering her lap.

The cabin is beautiful," she said. "I really do love it. And the fireplace. It's a good change for us. We needed the change."

"Even now? With my making you do this?"

"This isn't needed, Rick. You're crazy, wanting me to do it. But I'll do it. To show you I'm strong, I'll do it. And because you want it. Either way, I could love you more. Better now. Really. And I promise not to cry anymore. You won't have reason to get angry anymore."

She could not see him because of her hood, could not tell if he was looking at her. After a while he said, "If it's a good shot, Linda, he'll be dead immediately, before his legs buckle. It must be a good shot. That's all you've got to remember."

He had positioned them among the trees a few hundred yards down the eastern slope, near the tracks he'd found and watched for a week and knew that this was the spot for her first kill. He'd known it for days.

They waited.

Below them the fog searched.

The clouds moved and the rain slowed and the sun shoved little patches of heat only occasionally against treetops and down into the cold valley. The phosphorescent haze, pulled by the sun, lifted itself – seemed to breathe – and drifted slowly toward the west, penetrating the hilly regions of the forest, vigilant.

Lightning shot toward the sky somewhere behind and north of their hill and she jumped. He laughed quietly. She turned her head enough to see him gazing over toward the sky in the north, beyond the cabin.

"I like the cabin," she said. "I'm glad we have it."

He said nothing, turned his head back to the trail below. She looked down there with him, rubbed her knees with both hands.

"He'll be moving now," he said, and lifted his poncho to check the gun. "And he'll sense us if we let him."

"How do we stop that?"

"We don't. It's better for the game if he stays alert and afraid and uncertain."

"Oh ... the game."

She turned her head, looked back down the hill. The fog had pulled itself up from the basin and was hovering among the trees below them, waiting. She watched it shrug at her.

"I'll be a good shot, you know," she said. "As good as I can be."

He turned his head, sneered at her. "I taught you. You'll be good."

"What if I miss?"

"You can't miss. You aim good, you can't miss. Missing is something else you don't think about. When your arms are steady and you want the kill, you'll not miss."

"But if I do...?"

"Then he'll turn and run very fast and away and at a right angle to the sound." Rick gestured down the hill. "Then he'll turn again. But he'll be in the trees running. You won't get a good shot after that. I'll have to take him."

"He'll get away?"

"No. I'll be up and shooting before he turns the second time."

"You won't miss?"

He sighed deeply. A whisper growled in his throat and rose. His breath spat out as cloudy steam. He'd clenched his jaws. "If I don't think about that, I won't miss."

The rain had stopped. Linda watched the water drip very slowly now onto her lap. "I'm not sure..."

"I've taught you to hunt," he snapped quietly. "It's time to prove you've learned."

"But..."

"Just hunt good and honest and be a good wife without the fucking fear and wimpering," he hissed. "Do it now, so you know you can do it."

He pulled the hood back from his parka and swept a hand over his hair. She did the same, using both hands, careful not to make much noise with it.

The sun heaved its chest somewhere far away, beyond the trees and the hills.

The forest floor grew hotter – burned – and belched, and the black rot of a thousand ancient deaths pushed up from its throat, turning pieces of the silver fog to green, moving slowly up the hill among the trees. A gill, a claw, a weed, a gurgle.

"Stinks here," she said.

He smiled thinly.

They waited.

The fog approached. Eyes in droplets of vanishing sludge, silken hair on backs of wisps, searching, hungry, swimming in the mist, floating, chewing on the silver haze.

She watched it crawl up the hill.

"I was a good wife," she said. "I mean really good the way good is supposed to be."

"Yeah, well ... that's not changed. You're still good when you smile at me and mean it. You were good too back when you cared about us, when it was comfortable and we cared about things together."

"We could go back to the cabin now," she said. "And say that it's been proven."

"It's not over yet. You've got to feel the shooting, know in your bones how it feels."

"I don't care about this part of it."

"Stop that. He's an animal. Nothing less."

After a long silence she brushed the little puddles from her lap carefully and said quietly, "He's a man."

"What?"

She was silent.

The gravel rose from his throat. "A man?"

She brushed the water from her hood, shook it a little, blocked her face from him.

"A man?"

"Maybe he won't come."

He bent his head to look into her hood. She saw only his lips and his teeth, felt his breath. "A man?" His head darted away, then came back. "We shoot him, he's not a man anymore. Or is he just another lover? That'll make everything fine again if he's just a lover. Won't that make it all just fine again?"

She glanced down to the puddles on her poncho, tried to wipe them away. When she looked up, he was gone from her vision. "Maybe he won't come," she said again. She couldn't see Rick, but heard his hiss.

"He'll come. That's his trail down there. He's been coming every day now for a month or more. I know that. I've seen him many times. He's got no reason to stop coming now. He feels safe. It's become his territory."

She whispered something he could not hear.

"What was that?"

"Nothing."

"It was about him," he said. "You've got to stop thinking that way about him."

"It was nothing at all."

"You wish he'd never come near the cabin, is that it?"

"Stop."

"He'd come so close ... you'd got to know him, got to see how gentle and brave he was ... so noble, so majestic, so..."

"Please, stop."

He snickered. "He followed you here? You knew him before? Was he kind then, too? And brave and..."

"Please! Stop it. Don't make me hate you again. Don't get angry."

"But you see now, don't you? Why it's got to be your shot? So you feel the truth of it?"

Linda said "Yes" quietly, not looking at him, watching the fog squirm out of the muck, heave its chest and – taller now among the pines – crawl up the hill on hands and knees toward them.

The forest quivered, rustled in its sleep. A squish, a purl, a soft hiss, a crack.

Her head jerked to the sound. There. No. Shadows of shadows in trees.

"He's come," Rick said. He did not move. "Be very still now. Become the trees, as I've taught you."

She looked down the hill, to the fog – on its feet now – shuffling across the ground, then above the ground, floating, chest high now and rising, gentle breezes prodding it toward the right, the sun still far away but pulling at it, drawing it up. She clenched her hands and pushed them harder into her thighs and began to rock a little. Too slow, she thought, too slow.

"Be still now," he whispered again.

Little pieces of the sun began to filter through the trees.

A snap. Soft and waterlogged. Another hiss. A slog.

"There," Rick whispered. "Down there on his trail. Proudly. Gone behind that oak to the left and back behind that narrow pine the stags use to scratch their heads, where the bark is gone. You see it?"

"No." She watched the fog rise.

"Now. There. Coming out, checking the ground. His head is moving away, now back, looking toward us, now back again. You see him. You must. I know you see him."

"No." She smiled a little. The fog was up and even darker than she'd hoped, masking the shadows of the forest behind it, clouding their view.

"He's not stopping," Rick said. "Get ready. We'll stand when he moves behind the brake. He'll be going through that shallow marsh down in front of us. Less than eighty yards. A good shot."

They waited. The fog rose, began to thin. She saw movement down there but tried not to think about it. Thinking about it is where the shot goes bad, he'd said, and she'd learned well.

Rick stood slowly, looking first to where his feet would be, stepped once carefully to his right, then motioned to her. She rose quietly. It is very important to be quiet now, she thought, and took one step to her left and a little back. The top of the fog was at her chin. She could see over it and down into the fen, at the shards of sunlight settling on the bogs to the right of the thicket, and knew now she could not lie. She saw him. Majestic. Yes. Noble. Yes.

"Do it. Once," Rick whispered.

"She pulled the rifle up and hard into her shoulder, rigid, steady, as he'd taught her, finger near the trigger, ready, pulling him closer through the scope, finger on the trigger now, watching, feeling his pace, seeing his head. She fired.

She heard the quick *plish* of the bullet piercing the marsh as her target darted from the crosshairs. The fog jerked itself around them and now Rick was in it, down the hill two steps, now three, now thirty feet down into it, now gone, but there somewhere, and the fog swirled, thinned with the swirl, and Rick was in it, rigid, ready, taking her shot, and she turned back and up, running, turning, above the fog now but seeing into it, seeing Rick, her rifle up and swinging, looking for her shot, seeing it, firing, very sure and strong about it now and knowing it was clean. She'd spent no time thinking about it at all.

The fog jerked and swirled and fell, settled to the ground and bounced, and rose again, slower now, and watched her. Mites of dust from chiggers' eyes, motes of froth from gills and teeth, riding hair in yellow scuds, searching, chewing on the silver haze. It seemed to smile.

Rick's legs buckled. She watched him fall. Her shot hit him a little to the left of his right ear. She watched pieces of his skull explode up and out then fall into the fog.

I won't cry, she whispered. She'd made a tidy shot. Pure. And impartial. Cold. And detached.

It was over now and she didn't want to be there anymore. She needed the cabin now. And the fire. She felt very cold, but a new comfort slipped into her. It was over now. Rick was in among the trees, part of the fog now, becoming it, searching.

She didn't cry. All the way back to the cabin she didn't cry. She stoked the fire and put the water on to boil. She wanted to bathe but knew it was too cold now in the creek. Stay busy in the cabin now, she thought. That's the easy part. The hunting is for someone else. I will never care for it, although it is pure. And clean. So very clean.

She made the tea strong and very hot and filled their mugs. She pried the cover from the sugar can and wiped the table and then the spoon and set it close, between their mugs, then stoked the fire again and sat. In a little while she polished the spoon again and got up and wiped the table.

It was too long before he came, but she greeted him and managed a smile anyway, knowing it was strong to do that. She waited while he sat and sugared his tea and tasted it before she sat to watch him.

"It is cold. Out there, I mean," she said.

"Yes," he said, and smiled. "But you keep the cabin warm."

"Are your feet wet?" she asked. "Your feet should be warm."

He sipped his tea. "No. They're dry."

She watched him.

"I think I've been shot at," he said.

She looked surprised.

"On your way here?"

"Yes. About a mile away. South of here. In the bogs. Two shots. I ran."

"It's such a dangerous place," she said. "So much hunting."

"Your husband hunts out there."

"Oh. Rick. Yes, but he's safe. He's good at it. Very good. And clean about it."

She watched him sip his tea – gently – and saw his power, his nobility.

So majestic.

Still, she didn't cry.

5

Orville

He'd gotten all the dogs to yelping and howling that
first night he screamed. Had the window been
closed no one in this drowsy town or in any of the
isolated shacks scattered throughout the hills
crowding it might ever have even known his name.
One of Jack's scraggly bitches looking to find old
chicken bones behind the post office got to barking
first, then the old black and tan that used to live at
the town's corner picked it up. He never seemed to
move. Ticks swelled up like golf balls behind his
ears and he howled as if tired being alone and too
bloodless to move. The shrieks and yaps traveled
through the trees and up in all directions that night,
like some kind of urgent message, a proclamation,
the growl of a great new lonely wisdom. A desolate
sound, like somebody lost. It rumbled up to the
workdogs and passed to the wild dogs higher up and
beyond the hills. Echoes on echoes of wails and
forsaken cries bounced off the valley walls for hours
after he was born.

The dogs seemed to know: Orville Shell had come to life.

He was silent after that.

His mother's name was Harriet Shell and she died that night without a husband. He grew quietly and barely noticed. A tiny crumpled woman who walked her brush goats along the valley road took him in, raised him in that little house behind the feed store. Everybody here remembers her. She used to cut the tops off new grass in the high- wire clearing they ran through in the early seventies. They'd brought the line up from Antlers and through the valley to get to Quixado, for the development up there. She'd clip the grass with those little paper scissors kids use in school and fill a paper bag just before the sun came up. Anybody'd tell you. They'd be up there looking to shoot a couple squirrels and see her cutting grass to boil up for breakfast. Had almost no top lip, a tiny nose pasted on her face. Three and a half hands high, Jeeter used to say. She died last month, right before Orville punched Jack out front of the feed store, about six of us out there watching, the punch shoving Jack back off his feet into the alley. Orville walked down the road after that, didn't look back. Nobody saw him since, till this morning.

Anyway, what I was saying, the night the whole valley was turning in its bed trying to block out those lonesome howling noises, the night he was born, she went right in and picked Orville up, took him back across the road to her little house behind the feed store. It was more than two days before anybody found his mother's body. Folks up here mostly keep to themselves, tend not to notice each other too much till somebody dies.

The sheriff came, and Doc, then everybody talked about it for weeks after, decided a wild dog had got in and run off with the baby. They made a little attempt at a search but gave up shortly. That baby could've been drug anywhere into those hills, they said. A year later they were still thinking about it. Anybody saw a couple vultures circling, they'd ride up, check on it. The kid was four years old before anybody knew he existed, had lived behind the feed store all that time.

Bennie still talks about it, how he'd been damn glad to finally get his pickup across the creek all five times the road got to it, two of the bridges gone and the water up to the pedals after that four day rain. Driving out to Cracker's Feed Store, he'd say, that pick-up bounced, slipped and slid through the creek damn near sideways in both places where the bridges gave out. Most folks stay pretty much to themselves in these parts, don't talk much. But each of us in our little group here at Cracker's always had one thing they could talk about real good all the time, over and over. That's what Bennie talked about, sliding across those bridges after a rain. Folks just kind of wander off when he starts into it now. But that day was different. It was his first day talking about the kid. Most of the regulars were already here. Six a.m. He came in grinning.

"Wow," he said. "Got out without two-by-fours strapped to my boots."

We all laughed, nodded, drank Cracker's coffee.

Cracker dropped his feet down off the woodstove, eased up and walked behind the counter, said, "Well, it'll be dust again on the ride back."

We all smiled, knowing how true it was and liking Bennie, admiring him, a city guy sounding like he'd sprouted from the Oklahoma woods.

Cracker asked him, "Two bags, Bennie? Sweet? For the goats?"

"Yeah thanks. Who's that kid?"

Shorty and Jeeter had gotten up to get the sacks, take them to Bennie's pick-up. Cracker nodded to them and turned back to Bennie.

"What kid?"

"You got a naked kid out there looks like he's drying off on your porch, standing there wavin' at the cars. Waved at Stroud's truck just before I drove up. Waved at me too."

The men around the stove got up. We all followed Cracker out the door. Shorty's mouth was open, staring at the kid over in the corner, one hand on the column holding himself up, the other one waving at us nonstop, fast, like one of them music things, a metronome, a huge smile bent across his face. We all just stood there staring at him waving at us. I remember thinking we all probably wished a woman was there, figure out what to do.

The sheriff and Doc came up from Antlers again and everybody talked it over and agreed with Doc the kid was better off left with the old woman, that he was healthy enough and there didn't seem to be any good reason to pull his roots up. Just give the old lady some clothes that'll fit him, let him be. Least it'd be company for her, keep her head from flying away, he said. A couple women disagreed but Doc told them they could check on the kid now and then if they wanted.

So the kid stayed with the old woman. Nobody ever checked on him. If folks thought about him at all again, they seldom mentioned it. Somebody said when Jack heard about the kid he told 'em he'd known the Harriet Shell woman, talked to her sometime. He remembered her saying she wanted to

call the baby Orville. So that's what we called him.
Orville Shell.

Over the years I'd see him and the old woman
walking along the valley road with the goats when I
came out here to Cracker's. Then, when I'd be
heading home again a couple hours later, they'd be
on the other side going back. He'd wave at me. I'd
wave back as I passed, slow down a little so the dust
wouldn't get at them too much. At each little cut-
away private road they'd stop a moment and he'd
wave down it. She'd smooth his hair down with a
flat hand and they'd wait a couple minutes, then
move on. You can't see any of the houses from the
road, folks so set to keeping to themselves the way
they do here, but he'd wave anyway.

The older he got, the more often we'd see him,
standing by the feed store porch, waving at the cars.
From time to time I'd make a little box of stuff for
them, go behind Cracker's and leave it on their step,
a hunk of smoked ham, a few eggs, couple jars of
my goat milk, pants I didn't fit real good anymore. I
never knocked or hung around back there, though.
Don't know why. I suspect others did the same, just
didn't talk about it. Folks always liked being alone
around here, maybe figured Orville and the old
woman did too.

When he got to about twelve or so he'd be out there sitting on the porch more often, even before Cracker opened. He'd wave at us as we drove up, toss us that wide bent smile. We'd go in and sit around a couple hours, hear each others' stories again, see if they'd gotten any better. They hardly ever did, but we listened anyway. Something to do, I guess. Maybe it was better than staring at that 12 inch Motorola hanging up in the corner, the way we used to. Nobody ever spoke much when we did that. After a while he'd moved closer to the screen door. He didn't lean, just stood, waving like always did, his arm straight out to his right, the elbow bent, the forearm straight up, the flat-handed metronome moving faster now because the arm was longer. He'd grown and was still growing, waving at the cars and anybody who came up the steps. The bent smile grew with him.

Once in a while, when somebody came late, they'd see him mouthing the words he heard through the screen, moving his hands, bobbing his head, his eyes widening now and then as if it was him telling the story.

We'd all just smile back, nod at him as we went in and take our usual spots, shrug, grin at each other. Cracker decided: let him be. Let him make the move himself, he said. One May morning,

Wednesday, seven o'clock, Orville did. Guess he was sixteen or so by then.

He'd obviously liked the goatmilk, outgrown my denim coveralls. He wore no shirt, no shoes, no socks. His hair'd been cut crudely, almost bald in spots and here and there stuck up like tiny whiskbrooms, too long in others, but he was big and getting bigger. He could've been any of the valley's milk-and-steak-fed sons. I remember wondering who the father'd been, checking him out. Nobody talked about it, though.

Shorty was telling Bennie the best way to catch the big catfish up in the creek, that first day Orville eased the screen door open and slipped in.

He didn't look for a place to sit, just cruised among the aisles, checked out all the shelves, studied all the labels, stopped only occasionally to listen and smile at Shorty each time his stroll brought him back to the stove. Now and then he'd slow down over in the corner and move his mouth and work his hands the way Shorty was doing, then when it looked like he had it figured right he'd try it without looking at Shorty, move on back behind the aisles, mouthing the words, gesturing.

"You do it at night," Shorty said, "get in there maybe waist deep and somebody on the bank with the flashlight and a good club."

Bennie asked, "Ain't there snakes?"

"Sure there's snakes, but you know they ain't got beds right there. You know the snakebeds and the catfish holes 'cause you seen the creek dried up, you know the spots and the holes in the bank."

Bennie nodded. Raymond put his feet up on the stove, folded his arms, smiled, watched them both, mostly Bennie. Jeeter drank his coffee, watched Cracker restock the chew-tobacco behind the counter.

"You get down there and feel around for the holes in the bank, the big holes, where a twenty pounder got room to back in."

"Twenty pounds?"

"Oh yeah, Bennie. Maybe bigger. Only after the creek floods, just after the rains, before the creek starts rolling back. You get your hand down there and slip it into the hole, easy, slow and easy 'cause of them teeth. Way back in there. Now, catfish taste before they bite. He'll close his mouth over your hand, taste it, then open it again just before he bites. Then you gotta act fast with both hands. You grab the spines and the whiskers with both hands and..."

Jack threw the screen door open and strolled in, went straight to the counter.

He told Cracker, "Thirty pounds sugar, six cans hops."

Cracker turned slowly. "Howdy, Jack. Sure. Don't know I got all six cans right now. Nobody else uses hops much anymore. I'll order another case."

"Gimmee what you got, then." Jack turned, looked at the group and the sugar sacks behind Shorty. He waited. Nobody moved.

Shorty said, "You gotta get your hands back in there fast and grip hard 'cause he's gonna..."

Jack said, "Gimmee six yeast too, Cracker."

"...start fightin'. And he's twenty pounds 'at feels like a hunnert, once he starts. You gotta..."

"Jesus, Shorty." Jack went over, pulled his sugar sacks off the shelf behind Shorty. "Story got so old you had to get a yankee down here t'listen?" He laughed, took the sacks out to his truck. Nobody spoke. Jack came back in, asked Cracker, "You got my hops?"

Cracker had his head bent, writing it up, told him. "Whatever's on the shelf, Jack."

Jack said, "Jesus," and turned. Orville had come up two feet behind him. He smiled, waved at Jack, then turned slowly and gestured at Shorty to continue.

Shorty said, "Well.." and looked at all of us. Nobody spoke.

Jack shoved Orville aside and disappeared behind an aisle. We waited, heard him gathering the cans. He came out laughing again, heading for the door.

"A yank and a dummy too," he said. He looked back, shook his head, grinned. "You boys gotta be lonely, doin' this shit every day."

Orville smiled, waved after him.

Cracker puttered with his tobacco shelf again. Jeeter got up and went to the sink at the end of the counter. We listened to him rinse his cup and set it on the drainboard. After a while Shorty stretched, said, "Well, got a sow I got to check on." He got up and ambled out, held the screen so it wouldn't bang shut. "Beautiful day out here," he said. We listened to him walk down the steps. It seemed a long time before his pickup started and he drove off.

Jeeter said, "Lord. Almost forgot what I come for," and went to the back.

Raymond got up, said, "Yeah. Cracker, gimmee onc of them packs of Bugle." He counted the money out onto the counter.

Bennie got up, said, "Gotta get back. See you guys." He left quietly.

Orville watched their cars pull away. After a while he turned to Cracker, started to wave, then dropped his arm and smiled, looked over at me and nodded, walked out and down the alley and into his house.

The next day, Thursday, just me and Jeeter showed up. Cracker was behind the counter sitting on his stool, elbows on the counter, watching Orville sitting in a chair by the stove mouthing, gesturing at him. Orville looked up and grinned as we came in, got up and moved quickly to an empty chair, held the back of it, then moved another chair closer to his, moved behind it, held its back for us, grinned, gestured, moved his mouth.

I sat in the chair. After a couple moments Jeeter took the other one.

We watched him.

He held a finger up and got his mouth into a tiny bent "O" and widened his lips and opened his mouth and put his lips together and did that again and raised his eyebrows. His eyes got wide and he tapped a finger into his palm, then two, then three, then spread his arms out and up and brought his hands back together *slap!* and gripped them tight and brought them down fast and his foot up high and slammed it down *wham!* as the clasped hands shot down through the air. He leaned closer to us and put a finger to a tiny "o" at his lips. His eyes narrowed and one eye winked. He got up from the chair and hunkered down a little closer, his forearms on his knees, looking up at us, tapping his hand with a finger, spreading his hands and smiling slyly with his eyes as his mouth twisted, telling us a story no one could hear.

Well, you can imagine. Bunch of fools. Jeeter leaned closer, watched the eyes, the hands, the mouth. After a while, when Orville stopped for a second, catch his breath, Jeeter said, "Then what happened?"

Cracker laughed, came over, took a chair.

Me and Jeeter stayed three hours that day, listening to Orville.

We didn't understand a word he said.

About three that afternoon I went over, told Bennie while he did his second milking, told him go get Shorty. Jeeter found Raymond trying to wedge a hunk of wide hickory apart for his woodpile.

We were back together at Cracker's the next day.

Orville wasn't there. Nobody spoke much.

After a while Jeeter went back and found Orville in his house brushing the old woman's hair. The way Jeeter tells it, she was purple as boar's nuts and twice as wrinkled, three hands long now, layin' back like she was asleep, her mouth open and her tiny feet gray as dust. Her hair was coming out as Orville brushed.

The sheriff and Doc came out again and the sheriff looked at us and shook his head like he didn't understand something. Doc came out and told me she'd been dead about a week. I don't know why it was me he told. He could of told anybody. I never told nobody else. They hauled her off and most that wanted to stay got Cracker's stove going and some went and brought food back. Some went to Antler's and got greens. Snapbeans and spinach and green stringy stuff that looked like grass you couldn't grow up here. It was nice, what they did, how they all came out, away from their chores and their business of keeping themselves intact the way they did, just to comfort Orville.

Jack came by late in the afternoon, ate some and talked some, got some of the men over to his pickup, handed out a bottle or two of his newest brew. Some of the women pulled their men away the way they do and looked for Orville. Somebody cruised back the alley to the house. He wasn't there. A good crowd had gathered at Cracker's. It was hard to find him at first, everybody buzzing around and not knowing much, until Bennie saw him coming back from the edge of town, down the road. Everybody watched him come back. Some got proud and some whispered.

"Here he comes."

"Good old boy."

"Poor boy."

"That Shell woman..."

"Who's to take him now?"

"Boy's never been to church."

"He don't know how to live here."

"What about the Shell woman?"

"Maybe he'll find a spot."

"No. Never seen him at church."

"Be rough for him."

"Let him be."

"He'll find a spot."

"What's he got?"

"A dog. He's carrying a dog."

The closer he came the quieter everybody got. He turned at the crowd and smiled, eyebrows up, and went back the alley toward his house.

"The boy's sick."

"No. Two mothers died."

"What's he want with that mangy..."

"Dog's got six quart ticks hangin' off him."

Somebody laughed. The crowd started to thin a little, women pulled their men away, back up the porch and into the store. Some left quietly, got into their trucks and drove off.

Down the alley Orville was sitting on a stump pinching the ticks off the dog, squashing them with his foot, lighting matches, burning the ones he couldn't get to, deep in the fur, the dog limp over his lap.

Jack strolled back there with a beer. I eased closer, halfway down the alley.

Jack told him, "You got my dog."

Orville looked up, shook his head, looked back down, his fingers searching.

"Yeah. That's my dog."

Orville spread the fur, held it apart with one hand, struck another match across Jack's boot with the other, looked up and smiled, looked down and fried the tick. The dog didn't move.

I stayed where I was, said, "Hey, Jack. He don't know nothin' about your dogs. That one's been dyin' for two years. Your dogs come down here lookin' for comfort, hang around here lookin' to be noticed and then they die."

Jack turned, stared at me. "It's my dog. You got somethin' to say about that?"

"Yeah. Come out here." I walked back out to the road. Nobody was there. Most had gone home. The others were inside. Jack was right behind me.

"Why do you care about that dog?" I asked him.

"Nobody here cares about dogs. They work or they don't. You know that. They don't work, you let 'em die or you shoot 'em."

"So why you want to keep this one?"

"It's my dog."

"Then feed it. Feed the rest you got hangin' around."

He glared at me. "Orville Jay ain't got no business with my dog. Let him find his own dog and raise it."

I looked at him, studied his face, looked at his eyes.

I asked him, "Orville Jay?"

He rubbed his face with both hands, stared at me again.

He said, "That's enough for you?"

I told him, "Yeah, Jack."

He turned and went back, grabbed the dog off Orville's knees. I stepped aside. He tossed the dog into the bed of his pickup, had his hand on the door handle when Orville went for him.

Jack spun, pushed him off.

Orville went to the back of the truck, reached in.

Jack opened his door, brought his pistol out. I didn't have time to move. Orville had the dog across his arms now and was already in the alley moving away from us when the dog's head jerked. It was all too fast. I hardly heard the gun. I saw only Orville's back and his head, turned down and to the right, and the dog's head and shoulders hanging off the right of him. I saw no blood.

Jack still had his door open. He tossed the gun on the seat and got in, closed the door. Orville laid the dog down and ran back. His arms were in the window soon as the truck started moving. The truck bucked to a stop a couple yards away, but Jack was already out the window and in Orville's hands.

The first time Orville hit him he held Jack's neck with his left, bloodied his nose. The second punch laid him in the alley.

Orville stood back, screaming something we couldn't hear, poking his chest with a thumb, slamming it with both hands flat again and again.

That's the last I remember, the first thing comes into my mind when I think about that day. He walked down the road, turned into the valley road and that was the last I saw of him, till this morning. It wasn't the shot from Jack's gun brought folks out of the store, or the fight, if that's what it was. It was the dogs.

It started soon as Orville started screaming.

The whispery screams and howls spun up into the hills like quiet thunder, a sound death might make. A desolate, almost silent sound. The workdogs ran it up to the wild dogs, licking the message onto their tongues. The sound seemed alive. We stared at it, felt it creep into our bones. Then it ended. The silence bounced off the valley walls for hours after that.

But despite all that, the thing I see most, hear most when I remember it, is him poking his chest with a thumb, slapping it with both hands, again and again.

He didn't come back. After three days I rode up to see Tom.

"I don't know Orville yet," he said. "I know he's a kid and I know when he was born 'cause of all the talk down at the feed store that day after. Even Lucky howled that night. Never knew why till later. My wife got up and made coffee, woke me up, said something about new thoughts coming and leaving in the valley."

"You remember the dogs?" I asked.

"Oh yeah. Too many all at once. It must've stopped the deer."

"You never saw him up here?"

"I know these woods." He chuckled. "My wife thinks he's up here, smart enough to hide from me."

"You look for him? When you mark your shoats, you look for him?"

He didn't answer, tightened his gloves, adjusted his reins.

"No one's seen him in three days," I said. "Since he slugged Jack. You heard that, huh?" I looked into the woods. "You think he's up there? In one of them old cabins?"

He pulled himself up onto the roan, watched his dogs staring into the brush, jerking their heads back to him, then back through the trees again. Lucky came up, rubbed the scarred side of her belly against my leg. Tom looked down at her.

"He'll be all right," Tom said, and started the roan up toward the old logging trail.

I looked up through the trees.

That's when people started to notice Orville. Well, they didn't notice him, really, because he'd disappeared. But people started thinking about him. More folks started coming to Cracker's every morning, just to talk about him, even Jack. I guess we all wondered why Jack all of a sudden started coming in, sitting with us in our little get-togethers at Cracker's, but nobody ever said anything about it. Mostly Jack stayed quiet now, just listened. Nobody knew much about Orville but they talked about him anyway. Maybe they didn't have anything else to talk about anymore, I don't know. But they talked like they'd all known him pretty good all his life, better'n anybody, better'n the dogs, even. Like

Orville had become their pal now, after slugging Jack.

They'd all known Orville for years before he slugged Jack, they said. They'd been pals with him all his life, long before he did it. Orville was like that, they said. They knew him. He'd talked to them a lot. Orville was a guy that held back, 'specially when he didn't speak, they said. Charlie said something about Harriet Shell. They all agreed. They all liked Orville. Nobody ever liked Jack anyway. It was good Orville slugged him, they all said.

Then one day Jack didn't want to hear about it anymore, told Charlie to just shut the fuck up about Harriet Shell but Charlie didn't until Jack looked at him real hard and then Charlie shut up. Even Jack knew Orville would come back. Nobody knew when, though. Maybe Jack just didn't want to think about what would happen when he did.

So we all sat real quiet every day and watched the old Motorola hanging up there in the corner with the sound off and drank our Dr. Peppers and waited. Nobody wanted to leave now. Fogarty even stayed, shaking his head at Cracker every time the phone rang and Cracker waving his hand back telling him okay, okay you ain't here, and everybody knowing Fogarty's wife wouldn't ever call there anyway, unless it was to find out who else was there. Spellmann came in later and looked around and at Jack and at Charlie and decided he wanted to stay. He took his regular seat on the feed sacks and waited. We all sat there for the rest of the afternoon – about three hours – not talking much, watching the TV with the sound off and waiting for Orville to come back.

Spellman was the young guy. New. Knew nothing much about us. He said, "Where's that guy Orville?"

Jeeter grinned at me, turned to Spellman, looked at him for a moment, said: "He'll be comin'."

Jack stared down at his hands. Charlie walked around, gathered up empty bottles, picked cups off the drainboard and wiped them dry, turning as he wiped, keeping his back to all of us most of the time, seeing us in the mirror as he wiped, a little constant grin there keeping him whole.

Somebody else said something about Harriet Shell, how she always lived alone across the road, then died giving birth to Orville.

Jack didn't speak.

Spellman didn't either, anymore. He looked embarrassed and didn't know why. I watched the TV screen. Fogarty kept smiling at me over his glasses and at Charlie wiping his cups, looking in the mirror watching Jack stare at his hands.

Charlie was in another slow turn with his towel, picking up a glass, looking at Jack.

"Ain't nothin', Jack. Really. Everybody knew what she was anyway," he said.

Jack waited until Charlie was in his turn away before he picked his head up. His eyes were glazed. I watched him grind his teeth and stare at the back of Charlie's head.

"What was she like, Charlie? Tell me." His voice whispered, crawled up out of the gravel in his throat.

Charlie didn't say anything at first, cruised around and back again, wiped another cup. He stared at Jack and grinned.

I said, "Jack, Orville got a middle name?"

He ignored me. I'm not sure he understood what I was asking. I couldn't see his eyes. They were somewhere in Charlie. His voice got quieter. The room got quieter too, colder.

He said, "What was she like, Charlie?"

Charlie stopped his wiping, stared at him a moment more, then waved it off with a hand, the towel still in it. "Hey, Jack. Don't get your bowels in an uproar. Ain't nothin'. Don't worry about it."

And we all settled back into ourselves. We did that every day, some nights, talking about how much Orville liked us and wondering when he'd come back.

He came back this morning.

I'd gotten up and gone out to the porch to get away from Jack's brooding. The room had gotten heavy with him there.

I saw Tom's truck turn out of Five Bridge Road, moving real slow, swerving a little at first, then straightening, heading this way. A few of Tom's dogs were in the back, leaning over the sides. When it got close I saw Tom in the passenger seat. Orville was driving.

He pulled the pickup to the side and the truck bucked to a stop across the road. Orville loooked over at me and grinned. He stuck his arm out the window and waved. I waved back, smiled a little.

They got out and Tom walked around the front, crossed the road, and came up on the porch, spoke in his soft terse voice, "Howdy, Pete," and turned to watch Orville with me.

"Hi, Tom. You found him?"

"No. He knew where he was."

Orville went to the back of the pickup, reached one arm in and pulled out a black-and-tan puppy. He set it down at his feet. The puppy looked up at him. Orville grinned and walked across the road. The puppy followed at his heels. Tom's dogs watched them from the pickup bed.

Tom went into Cracker's.

Orville waved at me again and came up on the porch. We stood together and watched the puppy try the steps, fall back, try again, make the first one, then the second and the third. He fell back trying for the porch. I looked at Orville. He smiled, watched the puppy get up and look up at him and try again. A couple minutes more and the puppy was on the porch standing at Orville's feet looking up at us, wagging her tail.

Orville looked at me and smiled, raised his eyebrows and bobbed his head. He started to wave at me, then stopped it, stuck the hand in his overall pocket. He turned, opened the screen door and walked in. The puppy scooted in past him as I held the door.

It became quiet inside. Tom and Cracker carried feed sacks out to Tom's pickup. Jeeter and Bennie got up to help. Cracker said "Eight more" as he passed them. Raymond and Fogarty went to the back, took a sack each out to the truck. Charlie got up, joined in. Then the new guy Spellman. Orville grabbed a sack. I watched the puppy follow him down the steps and across the road and back and up the steps again. Orville never looked back at her. The puppy never fell. She was at his legs when he walked back in.

We all got into our spots again.

Nobody spoke.

We waited.

Orville had come back.

Jack didn't move. He stared at his hands.

Orville looked at us and smiled, started to wave and stuck the hand in his pocket, grinned at us. He looked at me and I smiled back, nodded at him.

I said, "Tell us, Orville."

Tom smiled and went to the door.

"I'll let you boys alone. Need to check my dogs. I'll be in the truck, Orville."

Orville nodded at him and Tom left.

Jeeter said, "Tell us a story, Orville."

The puppy was at Jack's feet, sniffing. Orville watched her. He looked around, held up a finger, winked. He slapped his chest with both palms, poked it with his thumbs, his chin up.

"You're Orville," Bennie said.

Orville's head bobbed, his eyes bright, as if saying:

–Yes, I'm Orville.

He made his mouth rubbery, twisted it, pointed to it, smiled.

Charlie said, "You got a bent smile."

Orville's head bobbed as he went through his motions:

–Yes, I'm Orville with the bent smile.

Then he started shuffling his feet, waving both arms, gliding back and forth in front of us.

"What's he doin'?" Raymond asked.

Jeeter said, "He's trying to fly."

Orville shook his head, kept moving.

"He's dancing," Cracker said.

Orville clapped his hands, nodded, kept moving.

Raymond said, "Dances like a chicken."

Orville's head jerked back and his mouth opened wide in a big silent laugh. He did all his motions again.

–I am Orville with the bent smile who dances like a chicken. I am Orville.

Everybody laughed, looked at each other, nodded, pounded their feet, slapped their knees. Raymond kept his toothless grin, looking around.

Jack stared at his hands.

Orville came up to me, pulled a dirty crumpled note from his overalls. He handed it to me. The printing was crude, wobbly.

"What's it say?" Fogarty asked.

I looked at Jack. It says, "I am not Orville Jay. I am Orville."

Jack's head jerked up, his eyes on fire. He looked at me, then at Orville.

Orville looked down at him, smiling a little. His eyes were calm. He nodded slightly.

"What's that mean?" Spellman asked.

We all got quiet again. Jack pulled himself from the chair and stepped slowly out of the group, walked to the door and went out. He held the door, eased it closed so it wouldn't slam. A couple minutes later we heard his truck start and pull away.

Orville took the note from my hands, stuck it back in his pocket.

"What's that mean?" Jeeter asked.

I looked at him. "Means he's Orville. The guy with the bent smile who dances like a chicken. He's Orville," I said. "That's all it means."

Jeeter scratched his head. "Oh," he said.

Orville smiled at me. I nodded slightly.

"Well, tell us some more, Orville," Bennie said. "Talk to us."

Orville gestured:

–Tom's waiting in the truck.

He nodded goodbye all around and left. The puppy followed him out.

Cracker went back behind the counter, straightened up the chew tobacco shelf. Charlie went back to wiping the cups and the drainboard and the sink.

After a while Raymond said, "I wonder if he'll come back."

"Oh, yeah," I said. "He'll be back."

Bennie leaned back, put his feet up on the stove. "I remember that day," he said. "I was the first one to notice him, standin' out there on the porch naked. It was after a four day rain. Two of them bridges washed out. My old pickup...."

I smiled. Yeah, I thought. Orville'll be back.

6

The Parakeet

Dawn slipped into the air. A gray stillness crawled from the rooftops as light gathered with dark. A high wind swept sighing down through the empty street and whistled against the windows and corners of the old buildings. The air was dry and hot and full of grit swept up from the streets and off the decaying bricks. It skittered along the sidewalk, found her, stung her face.

She pressed her back against the doorway, pulled her knees closer to her chest, tried to cover her bare arms and head with the newspaper but it was not big enough and the wind kept tugging at it. She opened her eyes. A lone pigeon, its head tucked down into jumbled, broken neckfeathers, opened its eyes and looked at her. After a few minutes she stood and looked up and down the empty street, adjusting her crumpled cotton dress. The pigeon stood and shook a little.

She was a gaunt, dried woman with wintry eyes. Her chin was short, her forehead high and topped with a mangled duster of brown hair.

The pigeon flew across her face and she jumped back. It pecked about on the windowseat of an old store across the street, stopped for a moment and looked over at her through the shattered glass then continued with its breakfast. She stared at it. Three small birds glided down from an upper ledge onto the street. They peeped at each other and peered at her, then flew away in a papery whisper. A lone horn beeped quickly blocks away. She cleared her throat and spit, rubbed her nose and walked toward the sound.

Two blocks down, the city was coming awake. Cars were clearing their throats and cranking up. She turned right. Light traffic began to gather and the diners and breakfast counters started tiny drowsy hums. The smell of bacon and perfume, gasoline and coffee hung in pockets. People ambled up to bus stops, checked their watches, spoke in low tones. She ran her fingers through her hair and quickened her pace. After six blocks she crossed another street, turned left and strode across the intersection. A car braked and horns honked. She kept moving, her head up, her tiny chin thrust out, her upper lip clenched gently in her teeth. She moved faster, loose and gangling, all legs and wrists and elbows. She came to a brownstone fourplex halfway into the next block and stopped suddenly.

She stared at a second floor window for a moment, then darted up the steps and into the building.

Her door was locked. She knocked. A younger man answered, fumbling with his tie. She strode in and went to the kitchen alcove. He finished with his tie and closed the door quietly. She filled her teakettle and put it on the stove and started the burner with a match. He picked his suitcoat off the arm of the flowered couch and shook it, brushed it a little, then draped it back. He glanced at her briefly and brushed his hair in the mirror. She got a small bowl from the cupboard and filled it with cereal and set it on the table. She poured the milk and checked her little rosebud vase for water and set it back at the center of the table, then poured her tea and sat down and began to eat.

He moved to the parakeet cage in the corner near the window and poured some grain into the tiny feeder. The parakeet twittered a few times, then was silent pecking at the feed.

"Where did you go?" he asked.

"Away from here." Her voice was a squeaky whisper, patient and even.

"You had no money."

"I have friends."

"Really."

"Yes. Friends who care."

He said nothing for a moment, then approached the alcove, buttoning his suitcoat, smoothing his collar.

"You might've been hurt out there."

She glanced up, stared at him a moment, then went back to her cereal.

"I have to go to work," he said.

She didn't speak.

"We can talk tonight when I..."

"That's not necessary. I was fine before you came here."

"Do you want me to leave? Move out?"

She didn't answer.

"I thought you'd be happier here while I'm gone. Sometimes I need to be away for days. I can't help that. The parakeet..."

"You didn't need to do that. I've been alone."

"Then what is it?"

She sipped her tea.

He watched her. "I come back."

"Yes. You do."

"I have to hurry. My plane..."

"Then go. You need to go. It's not your leaving and it's not your coming back or the time in between."

"I don't understand."

"I know."

"Do you want me to marry you? Is that it?"

Her head jerked. Her dry ancient eyes became fierce, alive. Then she looked away from him, got up and gathered her bowl and her cup and saucer and spoon and put them in the sink and rinsed them slowly.

She said something in her high twittering whisper.

"What?"

She turned to him. "You bought the parakeet because you thought I was lonely?"

"I have to go."

"You thought I was lonely." The dryness had gone from her eyes. They seemed to sparkle. She smiled. "That I did not have myself?"

"I thought only that you were alone. Maybe some company would help."

"No. You think someone like me would be lonely."

"I have to go."

"Go." She moved past him smoothly, over to her couch, slowly fluffed the cushions, smoothed the fabric on the armrest.

"Yes," he said. "I need to run. Tonight..."

"Tonight you'll gather up your things and go away. I'll be away until you leave. Go away and pretend you'd never come."

He went to the door, picked up his briefcase, turned to her.

"I'll send you checks," he said. "Every month."

"I'll tear them up." She wiped the mirror with the dish towel, rubbed hard into it.

"But you'll need money for the..."

"I'll need nothing," she said. "I have myself and I'll have the baby. We'll have each other."

The door closed quietly behind him. She fluffed the third cushion and stood up, looked at herself in the mirror, fluffed her hair, smiled. Then she ran and opened the door, ran and saw him going out, screeched, "Hey!"

He turned in the doorway, looked up at her.

"Take your bird with you when you leave," she said. "I don't want it."

She didn't change her dress or comb her hair or wash her face. She took only her key and a thin blanket and the half-full box of birdfeed.

The rooftops were misty with light, melting into the sky. The flame of the sun licked over the rooftops and inched down across the decaying brick toward her empty doorway. Her street was still empty. She spread her blanket on the doorstep, walked across the street, reached through the broken glass and sprinkled some of the grain over the window seat, then went back and sat on her blanket to wait.

7

Annie and the Mick

Thing is, nobody could ever agree what those last sounds were. They found the bodies, sure, four of them, in different parts of the park, one draped backwards over a low oak limb, mouth full of Spanish moss, but those guys couldn't have made those sounds, even dying the way they did, broken like that. Wasn't an animal either, least no animal anybody ever heard of. A big tom cat, somebody said. Yeah, two hundred pounds maybe, forty cans of Kitty Delight a day, sound like that. Bullshit. An eighty pound hawk a half mile up getting a wing torn off, now, that's a different story, screech like that, the screaming heard so far away, so back and forth across the trees the way it was, so fast, so...

Bullshit.

It was like God or the devil really went and did it this time, pissed somebody off real good, found their match, something finally got between them, and not a goddamn thing they could do about it...

~ 1 ~

She was hurting, drifting away, and tried again to open her eyes. It felt like somebody'd Super-Glued them shut. But it'll be okay, she told herself. They'd find her in time. They had to.

Yeah. You're supposed to cook soup tomorrow.

No, huh? Jeez. Maybe it's tomorrow already. The goddamn brain's not working real red hot right now. My cheek's frozen to the pavement. It's summer and I feel very hot all over. The cement's warm. I've not cried yet and my cheek's stuck to the pavement. It'll be alright. I'm awake. Everything will be okay now. Somebody'll find me. I'm okay. So very warm. I feel so warm and ... Christ ... wet. I'm all soggy. I've peed myself. Damn. Peed all over, up to my face. I'm all in my pee, so much of it. I'll be okay, except for this goddamn pain. Once the pain is gone I'll be okay. Just need to get these eyelids to work.

Big fuckin' deal you are.

She knew it was dark, even past the eyelids. But not like when she'd started to drift away and closed her eyes. This was the real-night-back-in-an-alley dark, she remembered, and tried to stay awake and hold onto that. She pushed her tongue out between her lips, dry except down near her right cheek. She slipped her tongue down and stretched it waa-aaay around the corner of her mouth onto the cheek. It wasn't pee. The pain was in her stomach, the wetness all over. She thought about that now, concentrated, tried to concentrate, tried not to drift away again.

She was on a slope, her head lower than her feet.

Yep. Good Girl. Keep it that way. Down there.

She wanted to laugh but stifled it, knew it'd make her tummy shake and the pang grab hold down where it hurt. Or up where it hurt? She laughed. The pain stabbed her again. Keep it that way? I can't move, f' chrissakes.

Keep the blood going downhill, into the brain. Then maybe you won't drift away anymore.

Okay.

Okay? Nothing's the fuck okay, smartass. Now what? Think!

Everything's moving out of me. If I try to stand, everything will run out. Gotta see what I can do here.

She eased her right arm down, across the cement. Her hand touched something. A trashcan. She pushed the hand around and past it, felt way down there, down where it hurt.

Not as much wet down here. It's all under me and in my clothes, in my face, around my cheek.

She slid her head in it, got unstuck. Her brain
spun. A strange metallic taste shot into the back of
her mouth and up somewhere through the back of
her nose. She squeezed her eyelids shut and tried to
jerk them fast, force them open. Nope.

C'mon girl.

She tried again, slower now, eased them up, and
up, wider, now wide open, and held them there,
waited for the water in them to drain, tried not to
float away. The wall was a foot from her nose. She
stared at it, into it, tried to focus. She was going
away.

*Think of something, Annie. Concentrate. That's
the trick. Don't lose it now, girl. Not now. What'll
they do without your vegetable soup? Come in off
the street on Wednesday night looking for your soup
and it ain't there 'cause you lost it all in a fuckin'
alley? They'll pool whatever money they got left
after a whole day out there, take whatever they ain't
spent on drinkin' and buy a sack of potatoes, boil
them up. Lotta goddam salt, if Harry cooks them.*

Spit. Harry?

She tried to move her other arm. It was bent
weird. Her hand scraped something rough and
wooden above her head. The arm didn't hurt. She
thought about that.

Dummy. It's supposed *to bend. It's called an elbow. Your arm's leaning against a fence, smartass.*

Now what?

Ain't doing no good up there. Get it down here, on the ground with the rest *of us, doll.*

Shit. Easy for *you* to say.

She pushed the elbow out and bent the arm till her hand was at her shoulder, slid the elbow down, tucked it close to her ribs, got the hand flat onto the cement. She maneuvered the other arm and got it up and did the same with that hand, got it flat. Her brain spun.

No!

She pushed her eyelids wide, clamped her mouth and held her breath. Her brain spun faster.

Jesus.

Wrong!

I can't do this.

Focus. Focus. Focus, goddam you!

She opened her mouth, let the air out, tried short slow even breaths. The wall got clearer. She saw the pores in the cinderblocks.

Think. Concentrate. Think. About anything. You're on your way, girl. Your hands are right. Ready. Think.

Goddam dress is ruined. Saw it every day for two weeks there at St Vincent's on the rack. Even hid it near some ugly stuff so maybe it'd be there when I got enough to buy it. Violets on it. Fuckin' dress is ruined. Blood all over it. My new dress.

Not *about the dress, asshole. About getting the fuck* up*!*

I don't know.

The Mick'd do it.

I ain't the Mick.

You don't want to see him no more? Sitting alone at his table in the bar?

He ain't never talked to me. The Mick'd never talk to somebody like me.

Oh. Bringing real fresh stewmeat every Wednesday, setting it beside your pot in the house kitchen? That ain't pretty fucking loud?

Yeah.

Now you're thinking, getting all that blood up there where it belongs.

She pressed her hands into the cement.

* * *

It was easy after that. It hurt, but it was easier now, getting out of the alley. All she had to do was think.

Keep thinking.

Today's... Monday. Maybe. *Murder She Wrote* on the tiny Motorola tonight, but nobody ever wanted to watch that. Pain in the ass being the only woman in the house. After they all get done talking about today on the street Louie'll talk about his days as a wrestler and Raymond'll cry thinking about the kids he ain't allowed to see no more. Everybody'll talk about something just to keep not thinking about the booze again.

But what pissed her off most was Harry's potato-and-water-and-salt night. That made her move now, made it easier.

Harry's salt soup with potatoes.

She kept that thought all the way along the wall, almost out of the alley.

The easiest part was collapsing on the sidewalk.

* * *

She heard things, couldn't move, relaxed her eyelids, listened, tried to wonder if somebody was boiling water for Harry's potatoes.

"She's dirty. Look at her fingernails," a woman said.

"We need to get help. She's hurt. Somebody hurt her." A man.

"How can you tell?"

"Look at her."

"She's drunk," the woman said.

"No."

"Yes. Look at her hands."

"So?"

"She doesn't belong in this neighborhood."

"But she's here. We need to help her."

"She's somebody else's business."

"How can you say that? She needs help. What makes you think she doesn't need help?"

"Ralph. She's not our business. Look at the dress. It's two sizes too small!"

Ralph took a few moments to answer.

"Yeah," he said. "Kind of tight, huh?"

Annie smiled, let it go, floated away.

~ 2 ~

Frank was in a drawer. Cold. A dead issue. No point thinking about him anymore, or worrying over him, if anybody had ever done that. He was nobody's business now. Frank was certainly and finally not Duffy's business anymore.

Duffy got lucky with his rides, made good time on the road back. Two days out of Los Angeles he was already through Baton Rouge. Three hops had got him east of Austin, then ten minutes by a fruit stand and this guy saw his thumb and pulled his pickup over, gestured through the rear window, Jump in the back. Duffy waved thanks, tossed his totebag in the back and hopped in, glad he didn't have to sit up front and feel guilty about not wanting to talk to the guy.

Frank had looked bad. Old. Just fifty, but older now. They'd been friends for over twenty years, punched a lot of shit together from Jersey to Oklahoma till Frank got a letter and split to see an old girlfriend in Los Angeles last month. Duffy kept on to New Orleans, found his spot and got settled in a little, then got the word last Wednesday: Frank had keeled over in a downtown bar. Heart attack. Ordered a beer and the seventy-five cent roast beef on half a roll then fell off the stool, his girlfriend right there.

The trip was sudden, but Duffy'd been there before, back in the late sixties, and knew how fast and cruel LA could be to a hitchhiker. This time he looked clean. Short hair to match his age and a clean tee-shirt. When he got the message he bought a white crewneck three-pack at Saint Vincent's Thrift, one to get there, one for the visit to the morgue, another for the ride back. The two dirties were now in his tiny bag along with Frank's brown and yellow herring-bone sports coat, fake leather on the elbows. Duffy'd worn it only once, to go to court. Frank had called it their "going to court" jacket. Dumb move, bringing it. Nobody wears sports coats in the south, least not on the road in early October. Maybe he figured to look presentable when he ID'd Frank's body, thinking maybe Frank'd somehow know Duffy was standing over him in their jacket and get peaceful. Maybe he'd thought a little about letting Frank get buried in it. Crossed his mind. Frank in their jacket six feet under.

The guy at the morgue smelled like dark cafe espresso with a touch of Madagascar cinnamon and downtown LA formaldehyde.

"You want his belongings?"

"What belongings?"

The guy pointed to a paper bag on Frank's white stomach.

"Pair of clean socks they found in his back pockets. A comb. 'Bout fifty-eight cents."

"Bury it with him. The shoes too."

Frank's shoes weren't worth taking. They'd worn out with him. Ready for the grave, just like Frank.

"You're not taking the body?"

"Takin' it where? I got a small room, tiny closet, share a bath down the hall. Just here to get a name on his toe."

The guy looked disappointed, shut the drawer.

Duffy asked him about the girl.

"What girl?"

"A girlfriend. There was a girl with him."

"I don't know. Thought you came to take the body."

"I came because you didn't know who he was, found my name and address in his pocket. I'm here. His name's Frank Snyder. No known relatives. No address. Liked watching *Green Acres* on his old Motorola, even had the tinfoil antenna workin' just right till somebody in Detroit swiped it all and he went to fuckin' pieces, decided to come out here to LaLa Land where it all started, maybe find his tv set. You get the picture?"

The guy shook his head, did a slow shuffle to his office, Duffy right behind him.

A page and a half about Frank Snyder. The guy shrugged.

"She finished his beer."

The jacket was still good, though, not ready to toss, so he'd carried it in the tiny denim bag the whole two thousand miles back again. Besides, sometimes on a rainy day it could smell like Frank. Made a good pillow anyway. Helped him think, like maybe a piece of Frank was in the denim bag, still trying to hang on.

Croaked at fifty. Jesus.

The guy who picked him up in Amarillo talked too much, made him crazy, all the questions. A couple hundred miles out of Albuquerque trying for Philly and sounding already lonely. Where you headed? Where you coming from? Used to box, huh? Look like a boxer, your size and all, your hands. The knuckles and the nose. I can tell. You ever boxed in Philly? Good city for a boxer. You won a few and lost a few, huh? Out of it now, huh? Young man's game.

"Yeah, mister. I'm out of the car now too. This is my stop."

"Ain't nothin' here."

"It's my stop. Thanks."

The guy pulled over. Duffy stepped away from the car.

"I'm fifty-two, two-sixty. Never fought in Philly. Never won a fight. It's what I used to do. Now I just try not to be lonely. Have a good trip. Get your radio fixed."

Somewhere and nowhere, in the Texas roadside heat, he'd sat on the shoulder, waited again, leaned back on Frank. Frank in the bag. No wind. The wing of a large bird lying with them in the dirt. One wing. Duffy looked up then caught himself, laughed a little, looked around, laughed again, out there in the middle of nowhere wondering if anybody caught him look up, like maybe looking to see a bird with one wing flying in circles.

Dumb, ditching the ride. The guy could've brought him to Oklahoma City. But the questions weren't worth it.

Still at it real good, Frank. Waiting. Waiting for tomorrow. Always waiting for tomorrow, huh? Jesus, it's hot.

Tell me how it feels, Frank. You get hot first, before the pain in the left arm? That's what everybody talks about, the pain in the left arm. Shit. I had that a lot, never worked the jab enough before I got into the ring, I figured. Doc told me to quit, I

quit. Told him, Yeah, I'm too old now, okay, so
now what? He told me, Get another hobby.

Duffy fell asleep with that, dreamt about it in the
roadside dust and woke with the first cold fall night
crawling over him.

"Jesus."

He grabbed for the totebag, started to unzip it, go
for the jacket, but hesitated, zipped it shut again. He
jogged in place a couple minutes then tried to build
a fire in the middle of the road, maybe get
somebody to stop, but couldn't get it going real
good, decided to walk it a while.

A guy heading for Austin in an old VW Beetle
almost ran him over then picked him up, talked
about his cattle all the way. Duffy felt squeezed but
stayed quiet, tried not to think about Frank.

Now that Frank was gone he could get his life in
order, maybe find a good young boxer to work, help
up the ladder. The kid in Newark was good, damn
near ready to start, but daytime was tough for him.
Work and school, the kid's family. A shame. What a
waste. Well, the kid had his priorities. That was
that. They did a few early evening spars, but never
enough to get a schedule around. By six Frank had
always already got their nights moving real good,
all laid out, first at The Wash, a few hours, maybe
till nine or when the college brats took over the

place, drove the regulars out. Marty's was always good for a few, especially on Fridays when everybody cashing payroll checks bought a round and laughed with them like they were part of the gang and sometimes got them something to do the next morning, unloading materials or restacking lumber, minimum wage. Grit's was always the final cruising spot, close enough to their personal spots, the wider doorways, the streetlights burnt out or already broken, yet far enough away from the winos and the flophouses they could get a good sleep after the laughing wore out.

Duffy was free of Frank. Things would be different. He'd find another Newark Kid, maybe a New Orleans Kid, and get on with his life, mend things with himself and get his life rolling the way he'd always planned it.

Now, in the back of the pickup, he leaned back, stared at the sky, his head on the tote-bag, two smelly tee-shirts and Frank still crammed into it, the sun not quite awake.

He wondered about the body, what they do with you when you die alone. They stick you in an oven then fold the ashes into a landfill, everybody's ashes all rolled up into one and shoveled out together so the saints get to sleep with the sinners, let God sort it out?

The thinking did it to you, Frank, all that wondering what it's all about, trying to fit it all together into one big piece. I wanted to forget it all, Frank, and you always trying to remember *everything*, even the *bad* shit, find some goddamned *meaning*, f'rchrissakes. Jesus, you pissed me off. What's it mean *now*, Frank, lying in a fuckin' drawer, fifty-eight cents on your white whiskey-bloated belly?

New knowledge brings new cares...

Shut up, Frank.

...pleated hands show the ripe of age...

You're laughin' at me, Frank. I can hear ya. Bullshit. You were fifty, Frank. Fifty.

... inept muscles twinge from the reach to a higher thing...

Fuck. I found you at two in the morning, Frank. Two in the morning at the bottom of the stairs. Couldn't make it up the stairs, Frank, ten years ago. It was booze.

... bedroom steps seem endless and much too steep to climb.

You never were shit for a poet, Frank. I never told ya, but your poetry stinks.

Better than that 'Ode to a centerfold queen' shit you wrote.

"Shut up, Frank. Your turn to buy." Duffy said it out loud, the wind still in his ears.

They'd stopped at a light. The driver in the next lane looked over at him. Duffy turned away, tried to get comfortable in the pickup bed, fluffed Frank in the totebag, leaned back again.

I got to tell you something, Frank. I never liked you. Really. You were always a pain in the ass. I always carried you.

You carried me out of the stairwell and up to your room. That was it. You could've left me there.

Then what? Have that hangin' over my head? No thanks. Anybody would of done it.

Thought you didn't like remembering.

I'd of remembered that, I left you there. Anyway, you'd of made sure.

How, if you'd left me there?

You had an eye open. You looked up, saw me. I didn't feel like you gettin' in my face the next day. I'd of had to knock you out real good then.

Like you did with Mirrielees two days later, fourth round?

Shut up about that. It paid for the room, got us on the road. Jersey fights are fixed anyway. Everybody knows that.

Duffy, it was you *that fell down.*

They put something in my water. I had him, next round, and they knew it, saw it coming.

Duffy...

Just shut up, Frank. You don't know shit about it, your head all wrapped up with fitting shit together, remembering shit, never lookin' ahead or seein' what's *now*.

The truck hit a pothole hard, bounced Duffy in the air a little, tossed him against the side. The driver yelled out the window, Sorry, waved and smiled through the rear window. Duffy smiled back, nodded, then got his big body snugged into the corner real good. The totebag had slid to the other rail. Duffy stared at it, looked away, then back again.

You don't know shit, Frank, all that remembering, all the time keeping it with you.

Frank was silent.

Yeah. Next night at the bar, that first time with you, you get going real good and I think, Jesus, what's this guy about? Hurt my head that night, all your shit, We wilt and proceed, climb, falter, climb again. Somehow we do it and look back, you said.

Silence.

Duffy slid over, grabbed the totebag, got into the other corner and stuck the bag under the small of his back, waited.

–And the looking back is all the joy, knowing everything that's gone is still within us.

Joy? Jesus, Frank. Remembering is...

–We are and have become what we are because of what we've seen and felt. There's no forgetting how we got here, or why we are. We lose pieces and get calluses where we broke then move on to spread the word.

I don't need to tell nobody. They can find their own way like I did.

–You got me out of the stairwell, Duffy. I'd been in a lot of stairwells.

I told you...

–And you sneak around, help people at the Mission, huh? Hey, how about Annie?

You don't know nothin' about that. You never came with me. You left, you motherfucker, had to go see some babe in LaLaLand. Now what happened? See? You don't know shit. A lousy poet and you're a drunk and you smell and you don't know shit about nothin'. Really, Frank. I never liked you.

–We are, and despite ourselves love it because of our molding. Then we pass it on, we teach. Then we die. We've made our point. Only the living look back and remember. Hopefully in both directions. The past is our strength to go forward.

You still stink, Frank. Always did. Maybe not now, but three minutes out of that drawer you'll stink like a bad turnip. Your poetry with you. And the clean socks. Fuckin' shame I let you keep your fifty-eight cents. Damn near half somebody's morning trying for a room tonight.

–Remember...

Fuck off, Frank. You're dead and it's your own goddamned fault. Today is today. Tomorrow will get here sooner than anybody wants. Yesterday's gone.

–The little red wagon...

Shut up!

The pickup got into Metairie and pulled over, dropped him off. The guy gestured, Far as I go. Duffy waved thanks. Airline Drive, four lanes, sometimes six, the airport five miles back. Motel row, where Jimmy Swaggart fell from grace. Early morning now and heavy traffic moving slow, headed for New Orleans, its heart maybe ten miles away. Too heavy and not much room to pull over, bad for hitch-hiking. He started walking with the traffic, his left thumb out, no longer counting on eye contact. Early morning people going to work, a girl across the highway walking with him – a dirty teeshirt and shorts so tight her legs looked white from the tourniquet – undecided about her smile but hoping to make eye contact with anybody driving in any direction, make a sale, get her breakfast, maybe pay half her room rent. Probably lived in the room for years. She smiled at him. He smiled back. Both on a mission.

Get another hobby? Jesus. I got *paid*, f'rchrissakes. I got in the ring, I got money. Not too many could do that, or would've done it for *any* money. Take the punches, take the money, I told him, then he says, Don't do it anymore. You do it anymore you get a heart attack, he says. Jesus, Frank.

The girl left him at the last big intersection, waved at him, turned back to do her rounds again. He watched until he couldn't see her anymore. A couple miles down the road the traffic lights got rarer, the traffic faster. A contractor picked him up. Another pickup.

"Downtown?"

"Yeah. Great. Camp Street."

"You need work?"

"I live there."

"You need work?"

The guy smiled. It was a good smile. That helped.

"Not right now. Thanks."

The guy nodded toward the dashboard.

"Take a card. I need strong men sometimes.
You're strong, age don't matter."

Duffy didn't like him anymore.

The guy continued. "Work a day, you get paid.
Cash. No taxes. Take a card."

Duffy took a card, got out on Camp Street, told
him thanks.

Bad thing is, you died alone, Frank. Caterpillar
Pat, too. People all around him but he died alone.
Good time to die, I guess, Mardi Gras, everybody
around you having fun and all. Guess Cat Pat just
shut his eyes and went on, took his own float.
Wasn't none of us other bums around him, though.
Scary, Frank. I don't want to go like that, tow trucks
and street sweepers and cops cleaning up the drunks
and trash and he don't move. Laid in that doorway
fourteen hours, I heard, shit in his pants and the rest
of him already stiffer than he'd ever been,
everybody steppin' around his legs and laughin' and
screamin', trippin' over Cat Pat's legs tryin' t'catch
penny-a-thousand beads.

First thing, Duffy figured to stick his head into
Sutter's Mission, see who's there and who ain't
there, see what's happening, what's cooking, but
that idea got away. Carl still hadn't got out of his
doorway. That was the unwritten rule: You get
yourself up and looking presentable before the

public gets there, before daylight gets rolling real good. That way the cops leave you alone and the business people don't get their bowels in an uproar believing it's your pee they smell and the city government folk don't feel bad about wondering how to pretend you don't exist. Tourists are year-round people too. They're important. Keep clear of the other year-round people.

Duffy prodded him with a foot. "Carl. Hey, Carl."

Carl didn't move.

Duffy stepped back, looked around. The other all-nighters were already up and moving, blending into the gathering everyday downtown street-life, early business people too, finding the first great parking spots. People at the corner watched him watching Carl till the light changed, then moved on, everybody used to this stuff, the street waking up. Carl wasn't moving. Duffy kicked him again, harder.

Carl groaned. Duffy sighed.

"Carl. You fifty yet?"

"Uh, forty-seven I think. Maybe forty-two. Not sure." He got up. "Jesus. Getting cold at night. You a cop?"

"You wish. Slice of baloney on white and a roof."

"Oh. Hey, Mick. I'm late, huh?"

"Yeah, bum. Get up. People lookin' at ya."

"They gonna take pitchers? My hair okay?"

"C'mon, Carl. Get your ass up. Go eat."

Duffy helped him up.

–Up the stairs, yeah. Then every fight I had to wipe the blood off, damn near hose you down. I never liked the blood. You got to quit trying not to remember the little red wagon.

I never told nobody about that. How you know about that?

–You'd hosed it down and polished it for days...

Shut *up* about that! It was an accident! I tripped halfway up the hill is all! Didn't think about the traffic down below, that's all. That's gone. Today is today is today is "Today is today!"

"Damn right about that, Mick," Carl said.

Duffy shifted the totebag to his other hand, walked Carl toward Sutter's.

"Shut up, bum. You don't know nothin'."

"I know it ain't yesterday. Ain't even tomorrow yet. I gotta get a room tonight, Mick. You got room for me?"

"No, bum. Get your own room."

"Jesus. Three bucks I could..."

"Three bucks you're in a doorway before the sun goes down. I ain't got it."

"Maybe I'll dump these goddamn shoes, sell 'em. They're killin' me. Too new. Crapper knew what he was doin', tradin' 'em for that sweater."

"Try some socks, bum."

"What's a matter with you?"

"Nothin'. You oughtta wear socks is all, carry a spare, the way you live."

"Maybe. Gettin' colder. Where we goin', Mick?"

"Where you go every morning, bum?"

"Depends where I wake up. Usually behind a dumpster someplace so the stink ain't so obvious."

"You're a pain in the ass, Carl. You know that?"

"Yep."

Duffy got him to Sutter's, found him a seat with some Icelandic fisherman on a week's layover. The cooking at Sutter's could smell better than the galley mess, you poke your head in. Depended who's cooking.

Duffy cruised into the kitchen. Ira smiled, nodded from his stove.

"Passing through?"

"Yeah. Just back. Who's cooking?"

"Me, so far. Breakfast. I guess Raymond for the day."

"Raymond? It's Monday, huh?"

"Yes. Haven't seen Annie since you left. Thursday."

"Who's Annie?"

Ira smiled, stirred his eggs, both hands.

"Annie's why you know it's Monday, Michael."

"Oh. Her."

"Yes. You bring stuff for her pot on Mondays. Remember?"

"Yeah. That girl."

"You got your friend squared away?"

"Uh-huh. Jesus. Raymond? Potatoes?"

"Soup, I'd guess."

"Ira, you know how old Cat Pat was when he kicked?"

Ira shrugged, dumped his load of eggs onto an aluminum pan with both hands, smoothed them out with the frypan.

"Late forties, maybe. Why?"

"Jus' wonderin'."

"A couple of people were here asking for you, Michael."

"Like cop people?"

"Uh-uh. Like knife people. Came in asking for The Mick, like they knew you."

"Two of them?"

"Saturday night. Then two different folks Sunday. Yesterday."

"Big guys?"

"Big enough, Michael."

"Jesus. What's that about?"

"Dunno. Hope it doesn't come around here again, whatever it is. We haven't got room for it."

"Knife people?"

A nod. "Made sure I knew that. Showed me. Scared me, Michael. I don't want them here any more."

"Yeah, Ira. Sorry."

Duffy went out the side door, got back to Camp street through the alley.

* * *

It was a small room, about ten by six, a bed, a closet with no rod, not deep enough to shut its door anyway if you wanted to use a rod and hangers. Just a closet to use if you didn't want to always look at stuff that really belonged in a closet. Shove it in and shut the door. Years ago each of the four upstairs rooms had been split in two, doubling the number of rooms to rent. They now seemed incomplete, lopsided. The lone window that remained took up most of the street wall and looked obviously off center and less comfortable than before it had lost its mate, when it was one of two proud eyes in its original ten by twelve sitting room looking down over Camp. People on the street at night looking for somebody needed only to count the eyes from the corner to find the right room to yell up at. Duffy's was sixth from the corner. An abandoned dresser, once probably a handsome piece of the original room, now looked squeezed and trapped in its corner. Four drawers, peeling veneer, yellow mirror. A single lightbulb hugged the ceiling. Bathroom down the hall, bring your own paper. Pay phone at the bar downstairs.

Okay, so it winds up like this, you in a drawer and me getting really fuckin' antsy about my future, no girl, no kids, no puppy chewin' up my slippers, this room like a coffin and no way out except to the streets. What you left me, Frank, huh? Like I got one wing now. I had a puppy he sure wouldn't leave me this to step in, Frank, I wake up tomorrow no tag on my toe.

One of us was crazy, Frank. I ain't mentionin' no names.

Duffy emptied his totebag – stuck the jacket in a drawer and tossed the tee-shirts into a corner by the door. He sat on the bed and stared at the dresser a moment, then laid himself down and shut his eyes. The street sounds, muddy through the closed window, died at the bare plaster walls. He didn't fall asleep for a long time, finally drifted off trying not to remember the little red wagon, woke up dreaming of it.

To Michael, nine years old, it had seemed a lot longer than waiting for his birthday to come around again.

"Saturday," his mother had told him. "You can do it on Saturday."

It was too long away and felt longer away every day.

"What is today?" he asked once each morning and sometimes later, after dinner. He needed to be sure.

"It's Tuesday," she'd say. "Four more days." Or Wednesday and three more days. It was all so unfair, waiting for Saturday, but he kept his patience because he was the man of the house when his father was away. He'd had the job for five years now – since he was born – and didn't want to blow it now, not when Saturday was on its way.

So he kept busy polishing his wagon. The real good one, red and white with thick plastic sideboards. He cleaned it every day, took the sides off and squirted them with the hose, wiped them real good with the rags his mother gave him. Sometimes she watched, smiled with him when he stood back to look at his work. When he grinned at her she grinned back, real proud of him. He was the man of the house.

Then, at last, she said, "Today is Friday. Tomorrow is Saturday. You can do it early in the morning, before the sun gets too hot."

He went to bed very early.

In the morning, just before the sun came up, he checked his wagon one more time, brought it around to the front door and waited. He didn't mind the wait now. Michael knew it would be the proudest time in his whole entire life.

His mother would watch from a distance, of course, because that's what mothers do. But he'd do it himself because he was the man of the house.

Today he would take his baby brother for his first ride around the block.

It was a most memorable trip.

He waved at all the cars on Wissahicken Drive. His brother waved too. Some people honked their horns as they sped past. He turned the corner at Rittenhouse street, leaned his body forward for the hard pull up the hill, toward home. And then one of the sidewalk sections sticking up a little from the others met his toe, a quarter inch that might have been a foot, or a mile, it might have been a wall for all it mattered 'cause now his knee was hitting the sidewalk hard, then the side of his leg and his hand

and now he was too far down to keep his body from going down further, moving itself away from the wagon, and his other arm couldn't make the stretch, and there was nothin' he could do, not a goddam thing he could do 'cause he tried, f'chrissakes, really, he goddamn tried, but the hand knew what it couldn't do, knew it couldn't goddammit hold on, and the hand was tearing itself away from the wagon now...

And the wagon was gone from him, on its own now, rolling back down Rittenhouse Street and into Wissahicken Drive...

...nothin' he could do...

I didn't mean itI didn't meanit Ididn'tmeanit

"I didn't mean it!"

Michael Duffy woke up sweating the most godawful sweat he'd ever done in any ring in any town he'd ever worked, with or without Frank watching him, taking him home, hosing him off. The sun was down. He'd slept through the day.

Downstairs, at Harry's bar, back at his corner table, the wall-lamp out, feeling comfortable again, first time in days, Duffy talked for four hours to the empty chair.

I don't mind tellin' ya we made a few mistakes along the way. You know that, huh?

–Yeah. Your deciding to bet our last thirty bucks on yourself in Raleigh was a bigee.

I ain't talkin' about me, Frank. Well, sorta. Besides, I had the guy cold. I coulda beat him next round, they hadn't stopped it.

–Right. Sixth round, you on the mat twice and them no longer able to stop the blood running into your eyes.

I'm talkin' about Camden. If I'd of stayed with ya at Jimmie Warner's drying-out joint another two weeks or so you'd of made another year. At least. We'd be on Lake Borne right now fishin'.

–Sure. You and me fishing. In a boat. Six days later some little kids under a bridge find our bodies and shit their pants.

You'da sunk, Frank, liver like yours. People'd be fightin' over the spot for months after, goin' for the crabs.

Duffy laughed out loud, shook his head. The four stragglers at the bar looked over at him, alone at his table. The bartender smiled, set them all up with one last drink.

"Last call again," he said. "This is it."

"C'mon, Harry," one of them said.

"This is it. Go home. Or wherever you go. Six hours we'll be open again."

Minutes later, Harry locked the doors, drew himself some Sprite and went over to Duffy's table, sat in the chair.

"It was your friend?"

"Yeah. It was him. Stuck in a drawer. Belly like a big round porcelain bowl. I'd recognize it anywhere."

"Sorry."

"Fuck. Ain't nothin'. Wasn't worth a shit. I carried him. Pain in the ass. He'd of had to find his own way anyway. Prob'ly best thing."

They sat with that a few moments.

"Just seems everybody's dyin' lately."

Harry got up, wiped half the table with his bar towel. "Maybe we reach a certain age we notice it better."

The ice machine made another pass, dropped its cubes into the bin and refilled itself.

"I need to get some sleep, Mick."

"Yeah. Me too."

"You want to do the floor behind the bar again Saturday? Nobody got it while you were gone. The pallets need a good hosing. You can do it on Saturday."

"Sure. I'll get it for ya, Harry. 'Night."

"'Night, Mick. You must be tired."

"Yeah. Road wears me out lately. Cold in here, Harry?"

"First cold for the year. Guess I'll check the furnace out tomorrow, get it rolling."

"Jesus. Coat and blanket time all over again. See you tomorrow."

"'Night, Mick."

* * *

Carl wasn't in his doorway. Duffy already knew all the spots. He found Carl's new shoes lined up nicely against a K-Mart wall and kicked the Kenmore refrigerator carton.

"Get up, bum."

No answer.

"Get up, bum. How much you got?"

From inside: "Eight inches and a lotta stories, new pair of shoes. You buyin' any of it?"

Duffy stayed quiet, waited.

From the box: "Dark in here."

Duffy waited.

A hand came out, picked up the shoes, pulled them inside.

"Get out, bum."

"Five for the shoes. Or a blanket."

"How about I set this box on fire? You been there?"

Carl scrambled out.

"Jesus, Mick, you don't play fair. You're crazy."

"Somebody is. You care about life?"

Carl sat against the wall in the dark, put his shoes on.

"Life? I love it. You woke me up scared. You're a heart attack, you crazy bastard."

"You're a bum."

"Yeah? News at eleven? What else? Bums need sleep? A flash."

"Cardboard, Carl?"

Carl got up, his shoes still untied, got close to Duffy.

"Yeah. Cardboard. A mattress in there I stole from Crapper before he ever got to Ira's eggs. Didn't like the shoe deal he gave me. A man can't get himself out of bed and out here into the shit, he don't deserve it. Better he croaks with the springs pokin' in him, give other people a shot at not turning stone cold in a doorway or a box just because they're too tired to toss in their sleep. I can eat anything. Finding a warm sleep's another story. Take's work. Skill. Some's got it, some ain't. I don't like it but yeah, I'll shove a stiff out, take his spot if he ain't up to it, he don't make it. Sleep an hour then take whatever he don't need no more, long as it fits me, then move on, keep moving, see if I can't find a better spot, maybe even find shoes that fit. Yeah. I do that and more. We all do it in our own peculiar ways. Even the uptown folks."

"Carl. Shut up. You got money?"

"A dollar eighty-seven."

"What you want? A bed or booze?"

"Both. And a woman."

"Let's see what we can do."

* * *

Duffy showed Carl his room.

"It's all I got," he said.

"Maid service? Pool in the alley, a hidden door?"

"Yeah. We get things rollin' real good, we'll buy an island, sleep under the palm tree."

"Only one tree?"

"Gotta start small, Carl, work our way up to a two tree island."

Duffy got a blanket from the closet, spread it on the tile floor, between the window wall and the foot of the bed.

"You're better here," he said. "That floor heater'll set you on fire."

"Thanks, Mick."

Fifteen minutes, Carl was snoring real good. Duffy drifted off half an hour later. During the night he got up, pulled the jacket from the drawer, stuck it on a hanger and hung it from a nail in the window trim. Then he got another blanket from the closet and draped it over Carl and opened the window.

Let Frank get a feel of New Orleans, three in the morning.

~ 3 ~

I figure it this way: You reporters write like you knew the guy but never even met him, never sat with him, never really drank a few across from him at Harry's, talked to the guy. He was always there, back in that dark corner, maybe wanting somebody to come figure it all out with him, but you never came. That's what I figure. Nobody ever figured it out with him or really got to know him and you write like you did. To me, that's bad reporting.

A friend

Letters to the editor
The Times-Picayune, November 11, 1998

* * *

Tuesday, October 27

Harry's was always thick-blanket dark. Twelve dim sconces along one wall helped find a table without bumping into it first, and a few red or yellow lights behind the bar made sure the bartender didn't poison anybody. The front door was always open. That got sharp sunlight creeping in a few hours a day, a little streetlight action at night, but other than that you were on your own.

Duffy and Carl had gotten up with the sunlight and shut the heater off. Forty-five minutes in the

bathroom, two guys had to go in, kick Carl and the
steam out, open a window. Duffy found him a pair
of socks and a clean tee-shirt ten sizes too big. Carl
put his regular shirt over it, 'Clean it when we do
laundry.' Now they were downstairs at Harry's,
Duffy's corner table, getting their entire futures
figured out over beers, Duffy suddenly looking very
weird.

His eyebrows were up, his eyes wide, round,
glassy. Carl watched him, bent closer in the dark.

"You say something, Mick?"

Silence.

"Mick?"

The eyes got black, inside somewhere.

"Mick!"

"What? Why you yellin'?"

"You alright?"

Duffy drank his beer. "Yeah. Whatsa matter?"

"Nothing. Just ... thought I lost you a minute
there."

"What you talkin' about?"

"My ears, I guess. The juke. Couldn't hear you."

"I didn't say nothin'."

"Your lips were moving."

"Bullshit."

"They were moving, Mick, nothing coming out."

"Crazy bum."

"Your lips were moving."

"Were not."

"Okay. My eyes and ears both going."

"Doorways and boxes. No socks. What you expect?"

"I'm doomed."

"Right, bum. On your way. Already got your pass. All the signs."

"The tight shoes, too."

"Yep."

"Years at the body shop, fixing people's dents."

"Yep. The dent doctor."

"You got dents?"

"Look at me."

"Fuckin' totalled."

"Graveyard stuff?"

"They wouldn't take you."

"Both doomed."

"Yep."

"Your lips were moving."

"Crazy bum."

"Your turn to buy."

"You don't get a turn?"

"I was in the head. Missed my turns."

Carl went for two more beers, Duffy's tab.

She came in looking lost, squinting, the sun behind her bouncing off fast traffic, four foot ten if you teased the boy haircut. The breasts had proudly started out to be breasts, made an honest effort and gave up early. Anybody's paperboy in a loose dress. Little Julie Harris in *The Member of the Wedding*. Probably in her twenties but looking fourteen. Clean sneakers. White socks.

Voice like a tired bullfrog.

"The Mick in here?"

Eleven guys at the bar. Half of them smiled, told her, Come in for a drink. Nobody knew The Mick.

Not yet.

She asked again, looked at Harry wiping a glass. Harry shrugged.

The tomboy eased a grin around eighty perfect white front teeth.

"Pulll-eeze, sirs? I really need to see him. It's impooooor-tant."

Snickers.

Silence.

From the bar: "I got Spic here. You want him?"

Short laughing.

She stepped into the bar, sat at a table against the wall, looked at Harry.

"I'll wait. Pink Lady."

Harry brought the drink, waited, turned his head while she fished the money from under her dress.

Carl dropped one of the beers, picked it up and slurped the suds, went back to the bar.

The Spic turned on his stool.

"Really, doll, hot stuff here."

Nobody laughed.

He got up.

A chair screeched, back in the corner.

The Spic, at her table now: "You lonely, mama?"

Silence, all eyes frozen at the mirror behind the bar.

Nobody saw the big bird flash across the room, or the claws that snatched him up and swept him out the door and threw him into the traffic. It was all too fast and dark with too much shadow in the doorway sunlight, but the Spic was definitely in the air and screaming and the bird already into the sun and gone when the Spic hit the truck, the cars now trying too suddenly to stop and not doing it real good all up the street again and again beyond their view but again Bam again Bam until they couldn't hear it anymore, the Spic definitely now between two trucks, the Spic and two trucks all locked together out front of Harry's bar.

Nobody saw the sun zip in behind them as the alley door opened and closed.

Everybody outside now, the girl gone, Carl brought the beers to Duffy's table, gave him one, watched him a moment.

"Your lips are moving, Mick. Promise."

"Old stuff ... slipped ... gone ... funny wagon smile..."

"Mick!"

Silence. Then:

"Crazy bum."

"You okay?"

Mick rubbed his left arm. "Yeah. A little headache. Why? You okay?" He drank his beer.

From the dark, behind Carl, the frog voice: "Hey, mister Mick."

Carl turned, looked at her, got up.

"Gonna play the juke, Mick," he said. "You got a quarter? Three for a quarter here."

Duffy gave him fifty cents and the hard shoes tapped toward the jukebox.

"Sorry, mister Mick," she said.

Duffy stood up. "You ain't botherin' me. Have a seat." He went around and held it for her, sat in his corner again.

"I don't mean that."

"What, then?"

"I gave them your name."

"Who?"

"The guys who did this."

She bent closer, fanned tiny fingers across the right side of her face, the eye and mouth, purple, the mouth corner still a little puffy.

"There's more," she said. "Down here." Her hand went below the table. "You want to see?"

"No..."

"They cut me open, Mick. Bad. I been at Charity since Wednesday. Just got out."

"Sorry..."

"Oh. Jesus." She threw her arms up, "Sorry, sir," tapped fists against temples, "Dumb dumb dumb," held out a hand. "You don't know me. My name's Annie."

He took the little hand, held it a moment.

"Pleased t'meetcha ... ma'am."

She grinned, all eighty teeth. Jukebox neon bounced off them.

"I'm craaaa-zeee, craazee fer feeling so lonely...."

"Ma'am, I dunno..."

"Call me Annie."

"Okay. Annie. I dunno what you're talkin' about."

"They cut me. The guys from Jersey."

Silence.

"I gave you up. Wouldn't tell them 'til they knifed me, but I gave you up, told them where you were."

"I don't..."

"Sir, they..."

"Mick."

"Yessir. They ... wait ... a guy picked me up on Airline, that's where I was working, we ... he paid me and that was that 'til he asked did I know a guy named The Mick, y'see?, a new guy to the area he says and it maybe looks like I know you but ain't telling him nothing and he don't like that idea or don't believe me so he pulls a knife and I tell him I never heard of you and he gets the other guys into the motel and they take me over to Old Metairie and..."

Duffy held up a fat hand.

"Now wait, wait ... wait."

She waited.

"These guys ... you want a drink? A Pink Lady?"

"Yessir."

Carl was already on it, brought the drink over.

"Wondrin' ... what in the world will I doooo...."

"These guys grab you, uh, pick you up, figure you know me. How they know that?"

Her shoulders bounced in the dark, head bent. Then, quiet, deep: "Maybe I talked about you."

"Oh?"

"Maybe to too many people, last few days since you came here.."

"Why's that?"

"Well, dammit sir I liked you, first time there outside the Mission, when you got here." Shrug. "Girls like us, we ain't got much to hold on to. I liked pretending you were ... mine."

Carl coughed, excused himself, went to the bar.

"And?"

"I guess word got around. People I meet, y'know? Told them I knew you when I really didn't. Just knew where you were is all, sir." The frog voice got squeaky. "I didn't mean nothin' to happen."

Duffy was quiet.

A squeak: "I gave you up."

"Ma'am..."

"Annie."

"Annie. You took those punches first?" He started to touch her face but pulled his hand back.

"Yessir."

"Mick."

"Yessir, Mick. Then, when they cut me in that alley I couldn't do it no more, hold out I mean. I'm sorry."

"Thank you, Annie."

They stayed quiet with that a while. She sipped her drink, leaned back, hands in her lap, looked around, kept her eyes from Duffy's face.

"I have often walked ... down this street before..."

"You know who they are?"

Duffy waited. "No."

Rubbed his face, both big hands. "Can you...can I buy you lunch?" Leaned forward. "I mean, are you okay?"

A little frog giggle. "Yessir, Mick. I'm okay now. You want to take me to lunch?"

"Maybe Sutter's..."

"Oh Jesus. 'Scuse me. The leftover Raymond potato and salt soup over bread special? Nossir, mister Mick."

Duffy sat back and laughed, deep down. The table shook.

He bent closer. She bent with him, neon on teeth, eyebrows up, waiting.

"I know the maître d'," he said.

If a bullfrog could giggle, that was it. She had it.

* * *

They did the back door, through the alley, Annie slow behind them, Carl antsy.

"Really. Look at this face. I wouldn't steer you wrong. Promise."

"Carl, it's in my bones."

"She's trouble."

"Shut up, bum."

Duffy gave the door his three slow raps. Raymond opened it.

"Hi, Mick. Hi, Carl. Hi..."

"You know each other, huh? That's Annie."

"Yeah. Annie."

Annie hung at the doorway, waited.

Duffy went back, took her hand, looked at Raymond.

"My date."

"Oh."

Annie grinned, more than eighty teeth, the nose a little bent, head a little up. She shuffled – sashayed – past Raymond, fixed her arm into Duffy's elbow, looked back at Raymond, did a little curtsy.

Duffy began. "Ira..."

Annie stepped ahead, nodded to Ira.

"Sir, we are here for our table."

Ira didn't flinch. "Yes ma'am. We have it ready." He bowed. "The lunch you requested is almost ready. Grilled honey ham and medium cheddar on white with mustard, a side of mushroom soup, ground pepper, the special Sutter salad with juice from the jumbo stuffed olive jar, no oil or croutons. Is that correct?"

She absolutely beamed.

"That is correct, sir."

"No potato soup?"

The suggestion destroyed her.

"Positively not, sir."

Ira definitely dipped from the waist.

"Your command, my lady. Your table is waiting." Ira gestured. "Raymond, please."

Raymond definitely sagged. He might have growled. No sound came out. He took them to a table in the main room, just outside the kitchen.

Carl tipped him a quarter.

It wasn't a big room. Once a '50s Walgreen's, somebody willed it to social services six years ago, before mid-city cancer could take its toll and condemned it to rubble. Ira sold the city his idea and a dying piece of Camp Street came to life. He wangled a bunch of free paint, institution green – for some reason the cheapest to make – and rousted the bums, offered free food for work. Most of them took pride in the work, finally having something to do that didn't involve getting spit on. A big section at the back became the kitchen, a storeroom and a bathroom, but most of the flat one-story building got kept for donated tables and chairs – pre-50s Toddle House formica and plastic and chrome – renovated with early '90s duct tape. Picnic benches. Church pews along the wall, more tables. Thick white coffee cups heavier than the barely three swigs you could put in them. Self-portraits and murals by homeless artists. A few donated or stolen neon lights and posters along the walls, Coca-Cola, Maypo, Fly United, *The Treasure of Sierra Madre*, *Casablanca*, *Citizen Kane*, Coca Cola again, a girl with impossible breasts holding a bottle of it, dripping ice somewhere on a desert island. No cigarette signs, no cigarettes. You smoke, you go outside. Ira's wife had died of emphysema.

Raymond picked four guys and the five of them filled the bowls and cups and water glasses, got folks seated and served and out in a hurry, made room to hustle somebody else through. Eating time was two hours, breakfast lunch and dinner. You missed, you missed. Tough titty. Next time don't be late. No hanging around.

Ira signaled Duffy, their special orders were ready. Duffy and Carl got the trays and they ate in silence. As usual, lunch got very noisy the first hour then tapered off during the second. By two the tables were clean and the place empty again, the door locked. An old man in a wrinkled suit swept the floor, six tables at a time, then a rest, then six more tables, Raymond's Tuesday helper, stretching his day.

They stayed quiet a while. Carl and Annie watched the old guy clean up and the street people pass and check the locked door, late for breakfast or too early and already anxious for lunch five hours away. Duffy watched Annie.

Appendix I

Notes on the Stories

Bennie

Bennie is me snapping to reality twenty years ago living on my own land deep in the Oklahoma woods. I'd hitchhiked 10,000 miles around the country trying to stay alive playing guitar and singing. That was a flop. I ran back to New Jersey and got a job singing at a local bar outside the Fort Dix/MaGuire AFB. That was a hit. The owner let me build to a quartet of friends I'd known from Philly. That was a gas, a smash. I loved it, saved my money and bought twelve and a half acres in the middle of the Oklahoma woods, cut a road through and pitched a tent, decided to raise registered dairy goats, thought I had it easy. I had a lot to learn.

Closing Up

I guess this one came from being alone with too many barmaids too late at night in too many bars. Jessie became a major character in *Salamanders*. A slightly altered version of this story became a chapter in the novel.

And some I worried over too much as I wrote them.

These too change constantly, sometimes daily, sometimes monthly, but I still ain't happy with them. Once in a while I go to sleep seeing the scenes and wake up in the middle of the night with an *aha!* that works and a lot of *aha!s* that don't. The answer's in my subconscious somewhere. I feel it in my bones. Meanwhile, I'll keep easing myself to sleep watching the scenes. That usually works for me.

First Kill

This is the first story I ever wrote, over twenty years ago. After that I wrote a scene about a man running through the woods escaping from something. I had no idea where I was going with him or what he was running from, but that offshoot later became Chapter 3 of *Salamanders*.

Orville

The Oklahoma woods introduced me to a lot of characters. I never understood the importance of "write what you know" until I'd left. Twenty years later, here in New Orleans, I stared at a blank page for days before realizing I'd already lived a handful of stories and seen a bunch of characters, me included. Orville is a fictional character. The characters in his story are a composite of folks I remember.

The Parakeet

I start most of my stuff with a scene, never really knowing where I'm going or when the story will end. Many writers disagree with that approach, but I've had fun with it. More important to me and my writing is trying to keep an objective narrator throughout the piece and not "tell" the reader how a character feels. Some of my fellow internet Writing Workshop folk didn't agree and sent me down here to the basement. That "cold idea" about writing was a no-no. I started this story mainly as an exercise to find out if what I believed was true, see if it was possible to create unwritten emotions, hit the readers with their own imaginations instead of a two-by-four. As the story grew, I knew where it ended. It's quick, still needs a little tweaking here and there, especially in the kitchen scene before they speak, but I like it. I'll work on it. Promise. Come back, watch my stories tighten up.

Annie and the Mick

[Editor's note:] The final section of this book, "Annie and the Mick" was written in 1998. Pete had intended it to be the opening of a new eponymous novel.

Appendix II

Notes from the Basement

Editor's note: Pete posted "Notes from the Basement" for an online writing workshop in 1997.

Basement Note #1

Hello, newbies, and welcome to the lists. You'll find it warm here and comforting, pleasant, soothing to your ... writing souls. I've been here since ... let me look at my wall ... since ... maybe a year ago. I live here, downstairs, past the room that holds the buried, still-warm treasured pumping hearts of still-born thoughts, just past that room, behind the blighted door and down the rotted stairs, down, past the archives, then to the left, down, beyond the crippled slipping sentences we've forgiven and misshapen ideas we've forgotten, down and to right now, watch your step. There. That door on the right now. Open it. Please.

Please open it.

Please...

Basement Note #2

Y'all're making me crazier, making me scratch my nose with my fingernails instead of my feet. I used a "which" today instead of a new sentence and even a "that". Before breakfast! (Lani'd come down with...ugh...milk and cookies and what was to *be* my breakfast scurried off.) At two o'clock I tried a "surmised", then an "eschewed" coupled with an "amid". My laptop blew up, couldn't take the redundancies, so I concentrated again on puntuation (hoping my pc up there wasn't crying), using the antique Tamera'd brought me with the beer and cigarettes. Things seemed to flow a little better after that until ... I'm sorry ... I started to critique you guys. Then all hell broke loose.

I critiqued about six or seven pieces. Felt pretty good, everything going along fine until...

You guys started critiquing critiques.

I started scratching my nose with my elbows.

Then my knees.

I'm back to my toes again.

You guys are crazy.

I didn't really think many people read anybody else's crits much. I was hoping they did. I think a lot of my crits are generic. Take what you need and leave the rest, so to speak. I read and crit line by line (obviously) without the distraction of what comes later in the piece. I figure sentences and initial impressions are what count. I piss a lot of people off, I guess, but my opinion has got to be sincere, even if their writing isn't. I think I've now learned, after months in this basement, what Hemingway meant by the author needing to have a "built-in shit detector," (carefully placing my comma *inside* the quote, where it should go, and continuing...)

Anyway, yeah, I think I've got one now, after years of reading and writing: A poop-alarm. I know poop when I hear it. Don't know why, necessarily, it's poop, but I "hear" it. If it walks like a duck ... etc. I trust myself to certainly know poop. Promise.

Put the comma anywhere ya want. I dare ya. It'll never sound the same. That's your business, sticking commas in, not your old English teacher's.

That's my "critique" spiel.

This is my "copy-editing" blurb:

The best anyone can do for their work is to have it "flowing" according to how they mean it to flow. Overlooked punctuation errors are death. I know about death. Ask my breakfast. They falter, they die. The *moment* – let me stress that – *THE MOMENT* the sentence falters, the flow and rhythm die. *Correct* and *well-planned* punctuation are critical to the painting. They're *as* important as the words, if not more so. The *paragraph* also falters when there is no rhythm in the sentences, no sense of the "sound" you want. Static is fine for tension, they say (though I often break that rule when I write tension, preferring sometimes the run-on sentence approach. It seems to make the quick image quicker), but you need an ebb and a flow, a widening and a "snapping" back. You can't just "write". (That punctuation is correct, the period *outside* the comma. You newbies shut your eyes. Apparently you're not allowed to know that).

One other thing. I ... oh ... my dinner's crawling over ... sheesh ... wish I had a dry match ... need to *cook* that one ... uh ... one other thing: I don't much care for the way you newbies are declaring yourselves as newbies every time you plunge in, take a stand. Y'all've been thinking and creating long before you got *here*. We ain't got all the news. A few over the months couldn't write postcards, so they left. We need you. We, combined, know a lotta shit, but don't know it all. Nobody does. We need you. We've all learned from everybody here and it'll continue.

Promise.

Basement Note #3

Uh ... one thing more. I'm starting to see a terrifying thread in the submissions to the fiction list here. Everybody seems to be "trying to write what they know." I guess that was a basic rule you learned from all the books. It's nice, huh? Yeah. A terrific and wonderful, pleasant idea. Beautiful. Inspiring. Close.

Crap.

Don't get me wrong. Your personal inspirations can sometimes create something worth reading about, especially with *your* writing ability. Awe-inspiring, unique, inspirational. I'd even stick "thought-provoking" in there somewhere.

Neat.

Colorful.

Unimaginative.

Huh?

Yeah. Come on. *Make it up!* The people, the scenery, the dialogue, everything! CREATE IT! Don't take it from your bedroom musings or your lonliness-at-the-office occasional sparks from the water-cooler gang. MAKE SOMETHING FROM NOTHING! Create. Use your imagination with words. You've read a lot. Now write. Just start with a sentence. Any true sentence. Make it up. "I know

as much about jogging as a chicken knows about
Shakespeare." Then proceed. Take it anywhere it'll
take you. It'll go. Promise. "Here and there he could
see patches of the dying Hickory tops that stood
their slippery ground knee-deep in the swirl and the
shiny reds and grays of the wind-soaked crags
looming beyond and only occasionally against
pieces of sky." That's the first idea I ever wrote
regarding "SALAMANDERS", my novel. I had no
idea where to go from there. I created that and the
other 90,000 words. That sentence is now
somewhere in the fifth chapter. Write a sentence.
Make sure it's "true" in all respects. (My apologies
to those who may think I'm "stealing" an idea from
Hemingway. Yes. I keep that idea deep in the soul
of my writing. Yes. I learned that from Hemingway.
Yes. It's a true idea, full of purpose.) Write a
sentence, dammit! Then write another one. Try to
keep everything the reader should *imagine* from
your sentences apart from the next one, try *not* to
write those "already imagined" following lines.
Instead, write the *subsequent* sentences *beyond* what
the reader might imagine, the images the reader
doesn't think about.

Listen. If I was a great writer I wouldn't *be* here. I
really don't know shit about writing at this point,
only what I feel. But I know writing when it's

wrong. I can read it and know. You can too, if you're objective about your writing. That's why we're here. If you're *subjective* about your topic, writing stuff you think's real to you but isn't, trying to write stuff *outside* your mind, *we'll* wind up being objective: telling you your stuff ain't worth the ten cents needed for a comfortable crap in New York.

Really. How's that for a deal?

Couldn't get it in Idaho.

(An aside: These notes were written last year. I'd been away from the north for quite a while. It apparently costs a lot more now for a clean stall in New York. Sorry for the "untrue" sentence.)

Basement Note #4

The narrow road crept meanderingly down around the little mountain toward the bottom where its dusty path was finally lost among the clustered houses.

It'd be comforting to know no one on this list would write that sentence. In my marrow, though, I think someone thinks it's good.

It doesn't matter how focused and precise the modifiers are. Using one in all – even half – the nouns and verbs can't help but make the sentence irritable, blur the image. The rhythm of a sentence must always alternate, however slightly, within it as well as in its paragraph. Sentences like the above example often make the reader's hair hard, his teeth hurt.

Basement Note #5

Fun? Yeah. I know someday I'll have a book of short stories to back up my novel. If I were an agent or an editor/publisher I'd push them both at the same time. That's what I'm aiming for. Right now, I'm content to keep studying and writing the stories. I figure about another year before I plop all this stuff on an agent's desk, all at once. In the meantime, I'll smile benignly at the rejections.

Basement Note #6

Plot is not necessarily mystery or suspense or tension. It's what the story is aiming to portray. If e.g. we have a character who has become desensitized to negative emotion, then any dialogue in the story *must* describe her movement (backward or forward) regarding that *particular* portrayal. If the dialogue serves only to describe generalities in her life and does not introduce *new* information about her change (backward or forward), it's static, doesn't move, serves no purpose.

Dialogue is where we come closest to the characters if the writer allows us to do that. We get to sit in that empty chair right next to them, hear them talk up close and across our faces. The character doesn't know we're there, but we are. And we *want* to be. We demand it. If the writer doesn't allow that, we'll leave the room.

So we hear it all. And watch. And listen. We don't want to hear about her gall bladder operation six years ago and her tryst with the guy in the garage. We're sitting there because we want to see how she's *changed*. Yes, even one day to the next. Yes, we nod, yes yes or No, please no, shaking in our guts, *being there*, *feeling* her not feeling.

We want that. Or we leave the room.

Basement Note #7

Something I remember doing years ago and still do to an extent, though now in my head only occasionally, randomly, often when the paper looks too white:

Keep a "bagfull" of sentences you like, short, simple, active sentences that describe senses (sight, smell, touch, etc.) or motions or scenes of any sort. Take them out. Detach the nouns and adjectives and verbs from each other. Toss them back into the "bag", shake them up, take out one word at a time and put it on the page. Continue. Continue. If nothing happens, you're dead. Sell your computer.

Basement Note #8

John writes:

>I've got to believe that people who are actually completing novels without outlines are ... somehow able to hold a plan, however vague it might be, in their heads while they are writing – perhaps even unconsciously.

Absolutely! Unconsciously (subconsciously) is the key word. I believe in this! It's possible to fall asleep thinking about your scene and (moments before waking up) dream it, see it, colors and all. Then it all depends on how much of it you can retain in you conscious mind, how fast you can get it down on a page. It's usually very fast, broad, the sentences jumbled, incomplete, adjectives and nouns and verbs all a jumbled mess, just so you can get the right ones, the ones you've pictured, instead of trying to remember it all in proper order later. The words, the images, the colors are what matters first. You also *see* it written in your dreams, *how* you write it, though that's hard to duplicate. It never turns out identical to the dream. Wish it were so.

Michelle writes: >What if the idea sucks and being stalled like this is affirmation that I'm wasting my time?

Everything is an idea. It's what you do with it, how you treat it, that matters. In fact, *everything* is art, depending on which view you take of it, how you describe it and in what terms. Picasso made art of lines he didn't draw. Orson Welles, at 25, made art of his broad vision of a man like William Randolph Hearst and a creative use of Hearst's sled as a metaphor for lost, severely missed, youth. The sled is shown seven times, yet disappears behind great dialogue and photography and direction until the end. I'd go so far as to say Dylan probably wrote a bunch of great lines, threw them in the air and, wherever they landed, that was the verse. Possible. Anything's possible. Anything is art. Depends on who's looking at it.

Rheal writes:
>Now, if only I'd spent that time writing instead of worrying about it, I'd be much further ahead!

See? Short and sweet.

Do it! This is not a thread about Pete or Jilla or Adrian or Michelle or Rheal or John or Craig Chantree or anybody else. It's about *you*. It's how *you* do it that matters. *You're* the only one can do it the way *you* do it. Nobody else. Y'ain't gonna write like me. Promise. Nobody wants to. And y'ain't gonna write like anybody else. In the end, it's voice. *Your* voice.

Look for your voice.

Find it.

Basement Note #9

Well ... I still believe outlining – despite its obvious benefits regarding "one-foot-in-the-door", "copycat", "this-sells-this doesn't" writing – hurts and stymies creativity and imagination.

Formula works, I guess. Unique is something else. As writers, maybe we need to become rich before we become unique. Dunno. I'll wait, maybe be broke when I die.

www.ingramcontent.com/pod-product-compliance
Lightning Source LLC
Chambersburg PA
CBHW051511170626
46811CB00002B/765